VANISHING ANGER

By
Gerald A. Moriarty

Strategic Book Publishing and Rights Co.

Copyright © 2018 Gerald A. Moriarty. All rights reserved.

No part of this book may be reproduced or transmitted in any form or by any means, graphic, electronic, or mechanical, including photocopying, recording, taping, or by any information storage retrieval system, without the permission, in writing, of the publisher. For more information, send an email to support@sbpra.net, Attention: Subsidiary Rights.

Strategic Book Publishing and Rights Co., LLC
USA | Singapore
www.sbpra.com

For information about special discounts for bulk purchases, please contact Strategic Book Publishing and Rights Co., LLC. Special Sales, at bookorder@sbpra.net.

ISBN: 978-1-946540-96-6

Other Books by the Author

Beware the Gaheena

In Search of Silver Wolf
(A sequel to *Beware the Gaheena*)

A Perilous Journey to Peace

Legend on the Mountain, the Legacy of Silver Wolf

Dedication

To Nancy, who has been the soother of my soul for forty-three-plus years, I dedicate this book. She has been my unwavering supporter and encourager during my time writing this book and all those that preceded it. To her goes all my love and thanks.

"I'm at peace with what time has given me.

—Gerald A. Moriarty, Author"

Preface

In the approaching years leading up to the 1850s, a young man grew into an extremely angry man as he worked the shipping docks. The docks were located on the East Coast in a large city. He made a bold decision that led him into an entirely new way of life than the one he had been living. While migrating west, he encountered not only skirmishes with several tribes of untamed Indians, but individuals of all sorts of lifestyles. One influenced his decisions greatly. He ended up in an area located near the edge of the great desert that some had called Death Valley. Many changes in his life took place as he journeyed to this location—his vanishing anger being the greatest one.

Chapter One

I'd had it with the worthless life I had been living, and I made a bold decision. I had been working the docks, loading and unloading ships. One becomes a different breed of person when stepping into that kind of life. I fought a lot and became quite proficient with a bale hook and the knife. The blade was my constant companion. I had left more than a few pretty bad off when I got angry from their constant badgering. I knew it was time to move on to something more challenging other than cutting a few coworkers up because of my short fuse. I had become a very hard and frustrated man. I needed to make a change before I spent the rest of my life in prison for killing someone.

I had a good horse, and was well armed with a .44-40 rifle and a .44-caliber sidearm. I was damned good with each of them. The speed and accuracy I had with my sidearm was well known. I was also dead on with my rifle. When I fired my rifle, whatever stood in my sights was dead. Also, nobody could outride me on a horse. This was not just bragging; they were verifiable facts.

After thinking about what I needed to do to get myself out of this mess that I had gotten myself into, I made the decision to head west. I began buying all the supplies that I figured I might need to sustain myself while out in the untamed area during my journey.

When all the supplies had been purchased and stacked against a wall in my tiny little shanty, I began the task of sorting out all of my belongings. I only kept the items that I figured would be essential for my survival. What was left I gave to a family who lived in the shanty next door to me and was struggling to make it in life. They were overjoyed. When everything was complete, I took a long look at all the stuff that was stacked against the wall and thought, *Now, just how in the hell am I going to get all that on my back and strapped behind my saddle? My horse would collapse.*

That's when I decided that I would need another horse to pack it all. I wouldn't settle for just any old horse. It had to be strong and fast with a load on its back. I had heard of one that a feller had up north a piece. I went up to take a look at it and was well pleased with what I saw. I bought the animal and led it behind my horse back to my shanty.

Now I needed something to pack all my supplies into. I went to a stable and told the man of my plans, and he fixed me up with an outfit and explained how to place it on the horse. He then went on and told me how to distribute the load. I became excited, as I was only a couple of hours from beginning my new chosen life.

When I started to place the packboards on the horse, he balked. He jumped all over the place. That's when I knew that I would now need a set of hobbles. I went back to the stable, picked up a pair, and then went home for another try. When I walked up to the horse, he stood there with a look like it was going to be a cold day in hell before I put those things on him. I reached down, placed one leg between my knees, and reached for the hobbles. The next thing I knew, I was hanging onto his leg and flailing around in the air after he reared up. I couldn't hold on anymore, and on my way to the floor, he kicked me a good one, knocking me over against the stall wall.

As I sat there I thought, *I just might have to make a few changes here. Dang, that hurt!*

I got up and dusted myself off. I studied that horse for a long time. I picked up the nose feed bag and placed some grain in it. The horse was watching that intently. As I walked over to the horse, he seemed to have forgotten all about what went on before. He stuck out his nose, sniffing at the feed bag. I slipped it over his nose, placed the straps behind his ears, and buckled it on. I deliberately left it a little loose so he would have to bend his head down to the ground to get the feed closer to his mouth. I thought, *I'll be damned! That's what those confounded women do to us men. They put a little food in front of us, and we'll just about do anything they ask of us. This danged horse isn't any different than us humans.*

As I watched, I thought I might be able to place the packboards on him. He didn't even seem to notice. I now knew the trick of not only placing the packboards on him, but placing the hobbles on him as well. I'd need to maintain a good supply of grain for the journey west.

I went into the shanty and began the task of bringing my supplies out and loading it into the pack sacks. When all was loaded, I saddled up my horse and led them over to my neighbor's place. I knocked on their door. The man came to the door, and when he opened it, I stood there holding out the keys to my shanty.

I told him that he and his wife could move into it rent free, and maybe it just might make things a little easier on them. I handed him a letter that stated if I hadn't returned within five years the shanty became their property free and clear. The note was dated and signed.

Vanishing Anger

He told me that his landlord had given them notice that they had to move out by nightfall. He said that this was a blessing from God himself. They both stood there with tears in their eyes. I told myself that I had to get the hell out of there before I started blubbering all over myself. We shook hands and I left.

As I rode off, they stood there waving until I disappeared from sight. That's when I took the corner of my coat and wiped the tears from my eyes. I thought to myself, *You damned old softy!* I rode over to the stable and purchased two bags of grain, and after loading it onto the packhorse, I mounted up and headed west. My journey had begun.

I was nearing the end of the wagon trail that was leading me west, when I spotted two riders sitting on horses stopped in the middle of the trail. As I approached, I recognized them as two of my ex-coworkers that I had not gotten along with and had cut up several times over the years. They had somehow gotten wind that I was leaving the area. The two of them were holding sidearms in their hands, yelling out how they were going to blow my head off for all that had gone on in the past. As they went to raise their sidearms to shoot me, I drew with lightning speed and placed new holes in each of their foreheads. Their guns fell to the ground.

They both sat there for a moment with blank looks on their faces, and then slid off their horses and hit the ground face first, not knowing what had hit them. I dismounted and commenced to strip them of all their valuables. When I was done, I dragged them off into the brush for a distance. I then tied their horses off to the rear of my packhorse. I thought they just might come into good use some day. Very few people branded their horses at that time. I felt safe, as their horses were unbranded, so I headed once again towards the west.

When I had reached my first camp spot, I built a low fire, as I was now in a territory with untamed Indians. I didn't feel like inviting them for dinner. I made a quick meal, and then began going through the saddlebags of the two thugs that I had killed. I found a bottle of good Irish whisky in each of the bags, along with several other items that I felt I might need down the road. I wasn't a drinker, but thought I might be able to use them for trading material along the way. I had removed their gun belts, picked up their weapons, and holstered them. They were now slung over the saddle horns of their horses. I thought that it might not be wise to let any intruders see them, and decided I had better pack them out of sight in my pack sacks. I took one of the sidearms and tucked it into my belt. It just might come in handy one day. Little did I know. I doused the fire and turned in for the night.

Chapter Two

Morning came earlier than I wanted. I made some sausage and small pancakes. I rolled the sausage inside of the pancakes and washed it down with water. I had never acquired a taste for coffee, so it made it a lot easier for me on the trail. I doused the fire and packed up for the continuance of my journey.

I avoided the Indians as much as possible, but there were times when you just plain had to go through them. Today was one of those days. I never had much patience for inconveniences, and these Indians were certainly an inconvenience. They had me half circled and well outnumbered. I had the advantage of being well armed and knowing just how big an obstacle I could get through. I knew that If I took off on a dead run I would take away the Indians' advantage, as they were not very accurate with their arrows when their horses were galloping full speed. My horses also were much faster.

I whipped my horse into action. As I did, I drew my sidearm and began dropping them as I went by. I hit a few of them, but many more followed. Now I was going to have to test the stamina of my horses. We were on a dead run and slowly leaving the Indians behind. I now just plain had to outlast them. As I topped a small rise, I looked back and saw that they were still coming. When I reached the bottom of the draw, I turned south, hoping to lose them. I rode another half mile or so, when I decided to turn back up towards the ridge. As I neared the top, I kept in the brush and trees to keep myself and the horses concealed. I didn't see the Indians anywhere. I knew I wouldn't fool them for very long, so I pushed on heading west as fast as I could.

When I noticed the horses were lathered up pretty badly, I knew I had to let them rest for a time. I spotted another patch of trees on top of another hill just south of me, so rode hard towards it. I entered the grove from the backside so as not to be spotted. I dismounted and tethered my horse to a tree. I left the others on their lead ropes, just in case I had to move out in a hurry. They wanted water, but I couldn't allow them to have more than a sip out of my hat from time to time until they cooled down. One by one, I removed the gear from them and gave them a good wiping down. I placed the gear back on them, and then moved on to the next one.

When I was done, I went to the edge of the grove where I had a pretty good view towards the north and east. I watched for some time, when I spotted the Indians topping a ridge heading back east. That was a relief, but I knew I wasn't in the clear by far. They may have left a few scouts behind to watch for me.

When I knew the horses were well cooled and fairly rested, I gave each a small bait of grain. I then let them drink a little more water than before. They seemed to be content and still in pretty good shape. I made a decision that once I was assured that I was in the clear I would set camp for a few days and let the horses completely recoup. I kept in the bottom of the draws and only topped a ridge when there was plenty of cover to keep us concealed.

It had turned dark and there was no moonlight to go by, so I picketed the horses and removed all their gear. I left their lead ropes on and tied each off to a tree. I gave them enough rope, so they could lay down if they wanted to. They would get much better treatment after the next day had passed, if it was without any incidents. Lord knows they deserved a break. They had sure proven their mettle to me. They were all strong and fast horses. In that, I was purely fortunate. In the morning, I was going to trade off my horse for one of the spare horses to give my horse a well-deserved break.

I settled for pan biscuits, jerky, and water, and then turned in for the night. I didn't even know when I fell asleep, as it came so fast.

When I woke up, I was shocked to see the sun was full up. Never before had I slept so long. I felt well rested, but I was angry at myself for sleeping so late. I didn't bother with a meal, and began packing up for the trek ahead. I stayed in the draws again until late afternoon. I slipped up through some trees to the top of a knob and looked around for any sign of life behind me. I saw none. That's when I decided to look for a place to set camp for a few days to rest the horses.

My stomach began telling me that I had neglected it, so I built a small fire and made breakfast. When done, I mounted up and began my trek west again.

About the time it was beginning to turn to dusk, I spotted a place that was well secluded, and I slipped over into it. It was the perfect place to set for a spell. There was a small stream flowing through it and plenty of feed for the horses. I stripped all the gear from the horses and gave each a good rubdown. They sure liked that. When I finished that task, I made a corral with my ropes and the ones that were on the saddles of the horses that were gifted to me by my ex-coworkers. I strung the ropes in a large circle that crossed the stream and back, so the horses could freely drink as they pleased. I was proud of my ingenuity. I removed the rope from the necks of the horses as I turned them loose into the makeshift corral. That put them even more at ease.

I then set up my canvas shelter and placed all my gear under it in case it rained. I then built up a good fire and commenced to making a meal for a king. It would be a steak with spuds and corn. Well, on the trail it was a meal fit for a king.

When I had finished my meal, I went to the stream and took a good, long drink of its water. I thought it tasted awful and wondered why. Once I was settled down, and before I turned in for the night, I went to the stream and took another long drink of it. It tasted even worse than the first. That's when I learned a pretty good lesson about placing the corral downstream from where I was going to get my water. When I looked upstream, I saw one of the horses standing in the middle of it emptying its bowels. Another one was urinating in the middle of the stream. I spit and gagged, and spit and gagged some more. It took half the night to get rid of that foul taste. I took out a piece of jerky and began chewing on it. That seemed to do the trick.

Things were going pretty well, after I had learned to take all my water from upstream from the corral. I stayed there for three nights. On the second night, I learned another valuable lesson. It was starting to rain, so I slipped waterproof capes over all the horses and myself. I turned in for the night. In the middle of the night, I awoke to laying in about three inches of water. The lesson I learned was that you never make camp near the edge of a stream, as when it rains, the stream will rise. It took all day to dry everything out. All those damned nags were doing was standing there with a snickering look on their mugs. I thought, *I'll get even with you damned animals.*

After rising on the fourth day, I decided the horses were ready to begin the trek again. I packed, and after mounting up I rode on towards the west.

I stayed low in the draws, and only peeked out on top of a knob when I wanted to check out my surroundings. On my third day back on the trail west, I encountered a small hunting party of Indians. They had me surrounded and wanted my horses. I wouldn't give them up, and decided to try something to see if it might swing their minds in another direction. I dismounted, and that spooked them a little. They all backed away a short distance and studied my every move. I walked back to one of my spare horses and reached in for one of the bottles of whisky. When they saw that, everything changed. I walked towards the one that I felt was their leader, pulled the cork out of the bottle, and handed it to him. He held the bottle up in the air and let out a war whoop that scared the hell out of me. I walked back to my horse and mounted up. I raised my hand in what had been known as the sign of peace to the Indians. I then slowly rode on out of the ring of Indians.

As I rode off, they didn't follow. I was relieved. All of a sudden, I heard their war cry again, but this time it was all of them. I thought they were coming after me, so I spurred the horses on as fast as they could run. I topped off on a knob and looked back. There they were taking turns drinking that whisky. They evidently had had whisky before and were really having a ball putting that bottle of it down. I felt it would be best if I put some distance between me and them before they sobered up and wanted some more.

I rode several days, making only short stops to rest up. I took short naps while the horses fed and drank. I ate while riding. When

I felt comfortable enough that I had left those Indians well behind, I set camp in a small grove of scrub trees. I picketed the horses and stripped all the gear off of them. I made a good meal and turned in early.

I was getting low on some of my supplies and wondered if I would ever run into any of the settlements that I had heard about that lay dotted throughout the territories as I headed west. The first thing I would supply up on would be grain, as the horses were beginning to become a little cantankerous because of how small of a treat I had been giving them to conserve it. I was out of salt, and that irritated me, as I liked salt on my meat. My canned food was also depleted. I was able to keep supplied with meat, as game was everywhere. I decided that I would keep heading directly west until I got out into more open country, where I would be able to see greater distances.

When I arose in the morning, that's exactly what I did. I continued in that direction for another four days. When I topped out on a large knob, I looked around at my surroundings. I spotted what I thought was a river out in the direction I was heading. I thought that if it was indeed a river, that it had to be a rather large one to be seen at that distance. I felt that, if it was a large river, there was a great chance there might be some settlements along it. That encouraged me. I headed directly towards it and would do so again in the morning.

It took another three days before I reached the shores of that river. It was so wide that I was afraid I might have come to the end of my trek west, as there was no way my horses could hold up swimming that distance with all that load on them. I made camp on a high spot along the shore. I contemplated on whether I would head north or south along the river in the morning to try and find a settlement. I felt there had to be one.

Chapter Three

When I woke up in the morning, I built up the fire and made up a steak for breakfast, as that's all I had left. I gave the last of the grain to the horses and loaded them up. I mounted up and took one last look around my surroundings. I felt that I had a better chance of finding a settlement south than I would up river.

Just as I was about to spur my horse down off the knoll, I glanced back over my shoulder and spotted something on the river. It was a great distance away yet, so I couldn't identify what it was. I felt I had better wait until it passed, and then make my way down river. As it neared, I could see that it was a rather large sternwheeler. The captain blew the horn a couple of short blasts. There were several deckhands standing near the rail on my side of the boat waving at me. I waved back. The sternwheeler maneuvered closer to the shore on my side, and the captain put the paddles in reverse to stop the boat. One of the deckhands yelled over to me and asked if I wanted a ride down river. I yelled back that I indeed sure would appreciate it.

The captain maneuvered the boat close to shore edge, and when it was as close as he dared to get, they lowered a gangplank over to shore and set it down. Two of the deckhands came down the ramp and approached me. I was nervous, as it was a cold reminder as to what I had left behind. When they arrived, they asked if I had anything to pay for the service, and I said I did. He told me that it would cost me three dollars up front. I asked him about the animals. He laughed and said they ride for free. I handed them the three dollars and headed down towards the ramp. When we arrived, they stripped all the gear from the horses, carried it up, and placed it on the deck. They then came back down and each took the lead ropes and led the way back up the ramps, with the horses following one at a time. I was the last to follow, and led my horse on up the ramp.

It was a relief when the horses were all penned up in the cattle stalls. I didn't think they would come up that ramp so easy. So far, they had surprised me a lot of times. The captain came down out of the wheelhouse and introduced himself to me. He asked me where I was wanting to go. I told him that all I wanted was a settlement that was on the other side of the river where I could resupply all my needs.

Vanishing Anger

He asked me where I was off to, and I told him west, as far as I needed to go to get rid of all the pent-up anger that was inside of me. He asked me why I had so much anger, and I told him of my experience of working the docks for so many years back on the East Coast. He said that he well understood, as that was what had brought him to this river. He invited me to the wheelhouse to have something to eat with him, and I accepted his offer.

While enjoying a great meal that I didn't have to prepare, we talked about our pasts. It was uncanny how our two lives paralleled each other's. The difference was that he still wanted to be around ships and I didn't. He tried to coerce me into going to work for him, but he didn't have a chance, as I pretty much had my mind set in what direction I wanted to go. He told me that he was sorry to hear that, as he needed some good trustworthy help and felt that I fit the mold. I thanked him for a great meal. He wished me success in my venture as we shook hands. I then went back down to the main deck.

It wasn't long before we were slowing to a stop. They were maneuvering the boat towards the far bank. It was a small settlement that I was informed had what I needed to get all my supplies.

The deckhands again went right to work setting the catwalk down on the bank of the river, and then returning to lead my horses down the ramp. After all my horses were offloaded, the deckhands went back and retrieved all my gear. Once that had been accomplished, we shook hands and I thanked them. They went back on board and raised the gangplank. Once it had been secured in place, the captain yelled out for me to be careful and if things didn't work out there would be a job waiting for me on his boat. I yelled back a thanks. He blew the whistle a couple of times, and then maneuvered away and on down river. It wasn't long before the boat disappeared around the bend. I placed all the gear back on the horses, and then mounted up.

I found a mercantile and resupplied all my needs. I bought ten pounds of salt, as I had hated it when I ran out on the trail west. I bought extra of everything, as I didn't know when I would find another settlement. I placed the extra on the spare horses. I was now ready to continue on in my quest for a place to settle. A new life! One that would give me a sense of solitude.

Once again, I headed west, sliding south a little as I did. I was now riding across terrain that was totally different from what I had just

Vanishing Anger

left. It was prairie grass as far as the eye could see. The country was so open that when you topped a small knoll you could see hundreds of miles in each direction. It was turning towards dusk when I found a watering hole that had enough to water and feed my horses. I decided to set camp, and picketed the horses for the night. At the settlement, they had told me that the Indians out this way were extremely hostile and to watch my back at all times. I made a small fire, made my meal, and when finished I doused the fire and turned in for the night.

The smell of food hit me in the snoot as I opened my eyes. I slowly slipped my .44 from under my blanket, and then cautiously turned my head towards the fire. I spotted an old man squatting by the fire with his back turned towards me while he was making breakfast. I thought to myself, *How in the hell did I not hear this man enter camp?* It was then that he spoke, telling me that he wasn't going to feed me breakfast in bed. He hadn't turned towards me as of yet, and again I thought, *How in the hell did he know I was awake?* I just told him that I liked my bacon crispy and my eggs over easy. I told him to warm the biscuits, so I could sop up the grease. He just squatted there chuckling. He dished up a couple of plates and turned slowly to hand me my plate. He poured a cup of coffee and handed it to me.

I sat up and just stared at the man. While holding the plate and cup, I told him that I wasn't a coffee drinker and handed the cup back. He just snorted and said that I would never grow any hair on my chest if I didn't drink coffee. I chuckled. I told him to give me the damned cup back. I slipped a slab of bacon in my mouth, and then took a drink of the coffee. He smiled. I thought there just might be a chance I'd live through this. I broke the egg yolk, took one of the biscuits, and sopped up the yolk and some of the grease he had poured over everything.

As I was staring at him, I noticed he was dressed in skins and furs, along with wearing moccasins. There was a large Bowie-type knife hanging from his hip on one side, and a large-caliber sidearm hanging from the other. He asked me what the hell was wrong with my eyes. He then asked me if I had ever seen a frontiersman before. I shook my head no. He then told me to get used to it, as I would be running into a few heading in the direction that I had been traveling.

I took my other biscuit, sopped up the last of the bacon grease, and then handed the plate back to him. He laid the plates in the fire facedown. After a minute, he removed the plates from the fire and wiped them out with a part of an old blanket. He did the same with the forks. He reached for my cup, refilled it, and then handed it back. I pulled my shirt open and looked down at my chest. He roared with laughter.

I thanked him for the breakfast and coffee. He said it would give us a good start for the day. I thought, *What the hell does he mean by us?*

He introduced himself to me. His name had been given him by a chief of a tribe farther west from us. He was called Long Knife. I told him my name was Randy, but that most people called me Rand. He told me that we were right in the middle of a couple of tribes that were all painted up for taking scalps, and we should get out as quiet as possible. I began packing. When ready, we walked the horses out to where we could see all around us. When sure it was safe, we mounted up and stayed low in the draws to keep as concealed as possible.

It was silent, and an eerie feeling came over me as we rode west deep down in a ravine where we were well concealed. We had been following an animal trail through the thick trees and underbrush. As we rode, it was noticeable that the ravine was becoming less and less shallow. All of a sudden, Long Knife came to a halt. He was looking up and listening for something. He turned his head and gave me the signal to be silent. After a moment or two, he began slowly backing his horse towards me. I was still pretty well concealed, and what he was trying to do was conceal himself. When he was beside me, he held up four, and then five fingers, and then held his hand above his head with two fingers sticking up. I assumed that he meant four or five Indians. We sat there silently for quite some time.

He slid down from his horse and signaled for me to stay put. He then creeped up through the brush on the hillside towards the top. When he neared the rim, he crouched down on his hands and knees, and then slowly worked himself over the edge and on out of sight. After quite some time had passed and he had not shown himself, I became concerned. I held out as long as my patience would allow, and was just about ready to ride on back towards the way we had come, when he appeared looking over the rim and letting out a loud war whoop like I had not heard before. He was holding something up in the air. I couldn't make out what it was.

He jumped over the edge in leaps and bounds towards me and was at my side in no time at all. As he stood there, he held up scalps he had taken. They each had feathers tied in them. He said there were five of them, but two got away. I wanted to throw up, but I held it back. He said we had better ride and ride hard, as the whole tribe would be back looking for us. We needed as much ground as we could get between them and us.

He mounted up and led the way on up and out of the ravine towards the north. We rode long and hard into the night. It was a wonder we did not run into another tribe along the way, as we certainly were not looking for any. Our concern was putting as much distance between us and that tribe he had relieved of a couple of scalps.

As we rode on through the night, we could see clouds forming towards the north and east of us. It was heading straight for us. We knew we would be losing moonlight, so we stopped and took out all the rain gear. We tied one over each of the pack animals, and then threw on ours. Once done, we headed west for any cover we could find.

The rain hit us just as it was turning to daylight. We had lucked out. Not only could we see to continue west, but, as an added bonus, the rain would wipe out all the signs that would tell the tribe where we went. By the time the rain stopped, we were so far away that the tribe would never be able to find where we had disappeared to. All they would know was that we were headed north. They would assume we were still heading in that direction.

Chapter Four

We came to a patch of greenery that looked promising for a camp. It was now beginning to turn to dusk, so we settled in for the night. The rainstorm had been horrendous. There now was a need to strip all our gear apart and dry it out. The horses all seemed to be relieved to be rid of the wet packs. After the fire was well on its way to being large enough to put out all the heat we needed to dry our gear, we spread it all out, surrounding the fire. We began the task of setting up our shelter and spreading out our bedrolls. Surprisingly, our bedrolls were still dry.

Our meal was next, as it had been a long time since our last one. I have to admit the coffee actually tasted pretty good. Once the meal was consumed, we took care of the horses. A small pool of water had formed nearby because of the rainstorm, so we led the horses to it and let them drink their fill. There was plenty of feed for them in the area of our camp. We wasted no time crawling into our bedrolls when we finished.

When I woke up it was well after sunup. I looked over towards Long Knife's bedroll and was startled to see an extremely large rattlesnake coiled up on his chest. I then looked around myself but saw none. I quietly whispered that he had a snake coiled on top of him, and he whispered back that he knew. He went on to say that he had known it ever since daybreak. He wanted to know how much longer it would be before I got the damned thing off of him. That was his mistake. I slipped my .44 out and took aim. Long Knife had his head turned away from me, so he couldn't see what I was doing. I fired, and it scared the hell out of him so bad he shot straight up into the air, flailing his arms and legs all over the place. I thought he'd gone loco.

Once he settled down, he screamed, asking where the hell the damned rattler was. He had a crazed look on his face. He was waving his sidearm all over the place. I thought sure as hell he was going to shoot me. I didn't dare move. I told him that he could get rid of his own damned snake the next time. I pointed towards where the rattler was laying. When he spotted it, he emptied his revolver into it while dancing up and down and all around. You would have thought he was standing on top of a whole bunch of those rattlers. The horses went wild and were jumping all over the place. When he settled down, I began

Vanishing Anger

laughing, telling him that he was really good at killing dead snakes. He looked at me, and then looked at his firearm and started laughing with me. He yelled at me, asking why the hell I hadn't told him I was going to shoot it. We really laughed after that.

I took a long stick, picked up what was left of the rattler, and tossed it well away from camp. Once settled back down, we made our breakfast. After packing our gear, we mounted up and once again headed west. I told Long Knife that I hoped all the shooting hadn't attracted any Indians. He agreed.

We looked for a high vantage point so we could survey our surroundings. As we topped out, we spotted smoke coming from a short distance away towards the north, so we rode towards it. When we arrived, we wished we hadn't. There were several mutilated and scalped bodies lying around near a burnt-out wagon. Several animals had been butchered. I rode over to the wagon and dismounted.

I walked up to the shell that was left, took hold of one of the wheels, and gave it a shake. What was left of the wagon collapsed. When I looked down at the remains, I spotted something that didn't quite look right, so I investigated further. I lifted one of the fire-damaged floorboards and spotted some gold coins. I gathered them up. It was just over three hundred dollars. I placed the money in one of my saddlebags.

Long Knife was several hundred yards away looking the area over. I mounted up and rode on over to him. He said that, in all probability, fewer than ten Indians had been involved and had left heading northeast. He went on to say that the Indians might have thought the shooting was coming from those unfortunate folks by the wagon. I asked if we should give them a burying. He shook his head no and said that we would just say a few kind words over them, and then get back on the trail. He felt that there may be other Indians in the area that might have heard the shots.

The remainder of the day was uneventful. That didn't make me mad. We'd had enough excitement for one day. The next few days were much the same. We could see mountainous territory off towards the horizon. It was more towards the northwest of us. I told Long Knife I felt that maybe that was where I would like to head. He told me that he was thinking about sliding more towards the south.

It was still pretty early in the day, so we stopped and turned towards each other. I told him that this was probably where we would

Vanishing Anger

He jumped over the edge in leaps and bounds towards me and was at my side in no time at all. As he stood there, he held up scalps he had taken. They each had feathers tied in them. He said there were five of them, but two got away. I wanted to throw up, but I held it back. He said we had better ride and ride hard, as the whole tribe would be back looking for us. We needed as much ground as we could get between them and us.

He mounted up and led the way on up and out of the ravine towards the north. We rode long and hard into the night. It was a wonder we did not run into another tribe along the way, as we certainly were not looking for any. Our concern was putting as much distance between us and that tribe he had relieved of a couple of scalps.

As we rode on through the night, we could see clouds forming towards the north and east of us. It was heading straight for us. We knew we would be losing moonlight, so we stopped and took out all the rain gear. We tied one over each of the pack animals, and then threw on ours. Once done, we headed west for any cover we could find.

The rain hit us just as it was turning to daylight. We had lucked out. Not only could we see to continue west, but, as an added bonus, the rain would wipe out all the signs that would tell the tribe where we went. By the time the rain stopped, we were so far away that the tribe would never be able to find where we had disappeared to. All they would know was that we were headed north. They would assume we were still heading in that direction.

part company. He said that he had enjoyed the ride along. As we reached out to shake hands, I told him that if things didn't work out for me that I just might drop down towards his direction. I told him he was a good dancer and would miss him. We laughed then, said our goodbyes, and parted company. I continued on in a direction that would bring me to the south end of that mountain range. Long Knife disappeared over the horizon to the south of me. I would miss his company.

It took the better part of a week to reach that mountain range. I stayed down on the lower elevations of the mountain until I had reached the other side on the western slopes. I spotted what I felt might be a small settlement off in the distance. I decided to make camp for the night, and then make my way towards the settlement in the morning. It was a little more south than I wanted to go, but I needed supplies. Time had been slipping away from me. I had no idea what month or what day of the week it was. It seemed the days were getting shorter, and the air was noticeably cooler.

Three days later, I rode into the settlement that I had spotted. I was in no hurry to get here. I found a small mercantile. They had all that I wanted or needed. I wasted no time supplying up. I found a man that did horseshoeing, and had all my horses reshod. I had been real fortunate that the animals had all stayed healthy. The shoes were extremely thin, and it had been a miracle that one or more of the horses had not thrown one or two. The ground had been soft most of the way.

Once I had taken care of all my needs, I headed on out towards the northwest. After reaching the base of the mountains again, I swung due west. I hadn't seen a name on that settlement, but it looked as though it had been there for a time. I didn't ask questions. Too much talk could lead to trouble, and that was the last thing I wanted.

It was a peaceful ride, and I noticed that I was gaining more of an appreciation for all that I was seeing as I journeyed on. I had been gaining more and more calmness, and all my pent-up anger had all but disappeared. For as long as I could remember, I had not felt this much at peace. I knew I had made the right decision. I was spotting more and more Indian tribes along the way. I steered clear of them. As long as they left me alone, I would do the same.

Once I had passed the mountain ranges, I swung north for a time. After a week or so, I swung back towards the west. I came to a fairly large river and had a lot of difficulty finding a place to cross. After traveling upstream for several days, I spotted a rider heading my way. When the rider got close enough, I could see that he was possibly a prospector. When we met up, I confirmed that was exactly what he was.

I had been looking for a place to camp. I asked the old man if he had seen a good place to cross with fully loaded packhorses. He told me that he felt there might be a place about a mile or more up river. I introduced myself, and he said his name was Piker. He said it had been so many years since he had heard his real name that he can't remember what it really was. I told him that I was beginning to experience the same thing. I told him that I had found out what month it was back at a settlement I had stopped at. He asked me what it was, and I told him that they had told me that it was October. He said that explained why the air was getting a little cooler. He said he was working his way south towards where the winters were a little milder. I then told him that I had better be setting up in camp before it turned dark. He asked me if I would mind company for a night. I told him there was no sense having two fires, so we set camp.

It was an interesting evening sitting near the fire. He explained how he got started prospecting. I told him that it just might be what I was looking for. He asked me if I had ever done any, and I told him no. As the talk continued, he asked me if I would like him to show me how it was done. I told him that it just might be fun. He then asked if I was in a hurry to get anywhere. I told him that I was just riding to somewhere and was in no hurry to get there. He said we would get started in the morning. After several hours more of swapping lies, we each turned in for the night.

I had a tough time going to sleep. It was a restless night. I laid there with the trail behind me racing by in my mind. I wondered if I was coming to the end of my search. I finally dozed off.

When morning came, the old prospector had already made up the fire and had coffee on. He offered me a cup, and without thinking, I took it from him. I thought, *Damn, I must be a regular coffee fiend now*. I chuckled to myself. When breakfast had been completed, we packed up and headed towards the river edge.

I spent the day with him as he taught me how to pan for gold. I landed a small nugget, and that got me hooked. I became pretty efficient at panning. He said he would show me what to look for when looking for gold in hard rock. The area we were in was located in-between two small mountain ranges, so we wouldn't have to go far to search.

The next morning, we packed up camp and headed back up river to where he said he had found a few traces of gold several days before he met me. Once we arrived, we set camp. For the next week, he showed me what to look for, to give me a better chance of finding gold. He showed me what iron ore traces looked like, and said that where you find iron you'll sometimes find gold. He went on to say that when you find gold you'll always find iron. He also said to look for quartz veins. That would be the most likely place to find gold. They were almost always found in a mixture of iron deposits.

He located and showed me a quartz vein that he had found before. He took out his pick and hammer and started chipping away at it. He picked up a piece and showed me a small flake of gold that was embedded in it. He then told me that there was so little of it that it wasn't worth fooling around with.

By the time the week had passed, he said that he had showed me everything he knew about prospecting, and now it would be up to me to find enough somewhere to keep me interested in looking for it. As we sat around the fire, he asked me if I would mind a traveling companion for a few days. He said he would lead me to where he thought we could safely cross the river. He went on to say that he hadn't done any prospecting on that side of the river and it just might change his luck. I told him it would be good to have a little company for a time. It was settled, so after a few more cups of that coffee I found myself beginning to enjoy, we turned in for the night. I figure it would prove to be a pretty interesting couple of weeks once we started across that river. I had now been captured by that danged thing called gold fever.

Chapter Five

When morning came and our meal was consumed, we packed up for our trek across the river, him searching for gold, and me searching for a new life. Two days later, we came to where he felt we could safely cross. We didn't hesitate. The horses balked at first, but finally gave in to our urging. The depth quickly took us to where the water covered most of my legs. I only hoped that it didn't get any deeper. Much to our relief, we began finding the water shallower. We finally emerged on the far side at midday. I told the prospector that I for one was going to look for a place to set up camp and dry out all the gear. He said he was in agreement.

It was a pleasant day and our camp was in a good location, so I asked the prospector if he wanted to stay for a couple of days and do some prospecting around the area. I told him that as we did we should look for a way up through the cliffs, so we could get out of the gorge. The walls were steep and high on this side of the river. We had crossed over into a bad spot. There seemed to be no escape, other than going back across the river.

We mounted up and headed up stream until we could go no farther. There was no way out in that direction, but we did find small traces of gold along the way. As the light began to fade, we headed back to camp. While sitting around the fire, we talked of whether we should take camp with us the next morning, just in case we found a way up through the cliffs. He felt we should.

Dawn broke the new day, so we made our meal. When everything had been cleaned up and packed, we loaded the horses, and then saddled our mounts. We looked camp over and were satisfied that we had missed nothing, so we mounted up and headed down river. As we approached a bend in the river where the cliffs were closing in on us, I spotted a draw that looked promising as a place we might be able to make our way up and out of the canyon. I told the prospector that if he would tend the packhorses and wait there, I would go up into the draw and scout it out. I spurred my mount towards that draw. I found what I thought might be an animal trail, so followed it upwards. It was in fact leading me through the tangle of boulders and brush, but did finally open up on top of the cliffs.

I rode over to the edge of the cliff to a point where I could look down and see the prospector. I gave out a loud shout and startled the old man. He looked up and shouted back that I was crazy. I turned back to the draw and descended to where I once again joined up with him. He told me that he thought I was falling off the cliff. I took the lead rope to my packhorses and led the way up and out of the canyon. The prospector told me that he was going to make a mental note as to the location of the crossing, saying that he thought maybe he would return and pick the area over more thoroughly. I told him that I would be heading west again in a couple of days.

We followed the rim south for a couple of days. Once we had settled in camp on the third day and were sitting around the fire enjoying coffee, the old prospector told me that he was going to part company with me in the morning and head back to that draw. He said that he had seen enough signs down in that canyon that there just might be a vein there that was rich enough to pay out. I think he knew more than he was telling me, but I said nothing. He was the prospector and I was the wanderer. After a late night of telling enough lies to last a lifetime, we turned in for the night. I fell into a deep, peaceful sleep. I really needed it.

When I awoke in the morning, it was full daylight. For some reason, something just didn't feel right. I rolled over in my bedroll and was shocked to see that the old prospector had already pulled out. Not only had he pulled out, but also he had taken two of my packhorses, along with my supply packs. I looked all around to see which way he went. I was so damned mad that all I wanted to do was find and kill that jackass. That was the last thing in the world that I thought that old prospector would do.

I saddled my horse and mounted up for the hunt. He had ridden off downriver. He then had made a wide swing west and circled back around where our camp was. It then hit me where he was headed. I spurred my horse to a full run. I only stopped long enough to give my horse a breather, and at each stop I ate a piece of jerky and a pan biscuit, washing them down with water. I rode on into the night.

The next day in the late afternoon, I arrived at the draw that led down to the river. I looked around for his tracks, but found none. I felt that he would be coming back to this location and I had beaten him to it. I rode wide of the rim, so I would not leave sign that I was on my way here. I brushed out all of my tracks that were near the draw, and then set myself up in a small patch of trees that was thick with brush. I had a great view of the area, and there was no way he could escape detection when he showed up.

It was late the next morning when I heard the sound of hoofbeats. I knew it had to be him. I waited until he was well past me, and then rode out behind him and called him out. He spun around fast and was startled that he was looking at me. I told him that not only was he a lowdown, sneaky skunk, but one of the biggest liars I had ever been around in my life. I told him that not only was he all of that, he was also a lowdown, dirty horse thief. He started out by telling me that he was going to bring them back in a couple of days after he prospected out the canyon. I told him to get off his horse and tie them off to a tree. He did as I told him. I then walked with him over to where the cliff edge was, while all the time engaging him in angry talk.

While we were standing there, I deliberately turned sideways, as though I was taking my eyes off of him. He dove at me. I sidestepped his charge, which left him standing with his back to the cliff. I drew my .44 and told him that he was now going to pay the price of a horse thief. He begged me not to shoot him. I told him that the only choice he had was to turn around and jump off that cliff. He screamed no, that that would kill him too. I thanked him for all the prospecting gear, and he again begged me not to kill him. I was merciful and shot him between the eyes. He fell backwards over the cliff. I gathered all the animals together, mounted up, and headed back to camp. When I arrived, I removed all the packs and gear, and then took care of the animals.

Once I had settled down in camp, I told myself that I would need to get rid of some of the extra horses when I reached my destination, wherever that was. I was now overwhelmed with them. I really would only need my horse and one packhorse. I'd use the others for trading. I went through the old miner's pack sacks and found a small leather bag filled about half way with gold. It was maybe a half of a pound. I thought to myself that the old prospector must not have been prospecting very long, or maybe he used some for buying his supplies. I never did let him know that I had those bottles of whisky. It then hit me that I better look and see if they were still in the saddlebags. They were there. I placed them all together in one of the sacks on my original packhorse. I settled back down and decided to have an early meal.

After my meal, I laid down on my bedroll and quickly fell asleep. I must have been mighty tired, as I didn't wake up until just as it was turning to dawn the next morning. I restarted the fire and cooked up some bacon and eggs, along with heating up a couple of pan biscuits. When I was done, I cleaned the skillet and my fork, and then packed them away. I loaded the packs and saddles on all the animals, mounted up, and headed out in a southwesterly direction, skirting around the base of a rocky mountain range, which led me in a straight westerly direction.

It was rolling dry plains for as far as I could see, and I rode for three more days before I finally spotted what appeared to be a small settlement off in the distance. It took me another day and a half to reach it. It was a small mining settlement by the name of Beatty.

The mercantile owner told me that some small deposits of gold and silver had been discovered in the mountain range to the west of there. I told him that I had some extra horses with saddles that I would like to trade or sell. He got excited about that. He told me that the blacksmith was always in need of horses. I thanked him, and then went out to my horse and loaded what little supplies I had purchased. I then led my horses over to the blacksmith shop. I found the blacksmith out around the back cleaning out some stalls.

When he looked up, he began beaming from ear to ear when he saw all the horses. Then, all of a sudden, he got a serious look on his face.

After walking over and looking the old prospector's horse over, he asked me where I came up with that animal. I told him the whole story, and he replied that the dirty skunk had run out on him without paying his bill. I went over to the packhorse, emptied all the packs, and placed it all onto my two extra horses. The old prospector traveled pretty light, as there wasn't much on the animal besides his gold pan, picks, and shovels. I then told the blacksmith that if he reshod my horses, he could have the old prospector's horse and packs. He told me that he would get right on it. That turned out to be a pretty good trade for me, removing all chances of an argument with the blacksmith over the horse and gear.

When the blacksmith finished shoeing the horses, I asked him if he knew of anybody that needed a horse and saddle. He told me that he did, and wanted to know which one. He walked over and looked the horse over, and then turned to me and said that he could get me a hundred dollars in gold for it. I told him that I would take it. Again, it brought a big grin to his face. He was probably going to get a pretty good profit out of that. He gave me the gold. I then said my thanks and mounted up and left.

On the way out of the settlement, I ran into a prospector walking while leading a donkey into town. I asked him which way he had come from. He just stood there staring at me. I then said that I was wondering if he knew of a good way over the mountain range that was to the west of there. He seemed to relax a little, and then told me of a well-used trail that would lead me to a settlement by the name of Lone Pine that was located west of the mountain range.

He then asked me if I would be interested in parting with one of my horses. I said I might. He said he would give me two hundred dollars in gold for the horse and saddle. He just bought himself a horse and saddle. I thought, *That dirty scoundrel of a blacksmith swindled me. I should ride back and put a bullet in him. Oh well, if I was dumb enough to fall for it I deserve to be swindled.*

I emptied everything and loaded it all onto the other packhorse. Its load was now becoming quite heavy. When the prospector saw me move the bottles of whisky from one pack sack over to one that was draped over the saddle, he told me he would give me another fifty dollars in gold for a bottle of whisky. I now had one less bottle of whisky. I still had two. That tribe of Indians back east had relieved me of one. I mounted up and headed for the trail that would lead me over the mountain. I set camp at the base of the mountain at the trailhead.

Chapter Six

When morning arrived, I stoked up the fire, made breakfast, ate, packed up, and after mounting up, headed up that trail. The mountain range had been given the name of the Amargosas. It were a jagged-looking range. I suspect they had been given that name by a tribe of Indians. The trail I was on was probably one of only a few places that one could safely cross. My guess was that it was the safest one by far, as well-worn as it was.

As I rode upwards, I could see pockmarks where prospectors had dug hoping to find their stake. It was a yellowish dirt that seemed to ooze out of the ground. The closer I came to the crest, the more pockmarks there were. I crested the ridge in the late afternoon. I spotted diggings everywhere. I didn't hesitate to begin my descent. The pockmarks were fewer and fewer as I moved farther away from the crest. I knew that it would also translate into fewer people. That made me feel better.

I was perhaps a third of the way down the mountain range when I spotted a nice place for a camp, so I set down for the night. It turned dark just as I finished setting up camp and taking care of the horses. There was a fairly good spring just a few yards from my camp, which made it even more comfortable. Feed was all around for the horses. I picketed all the horses close enough to the spring so they could drink as they desired, and with all the greenery around the spring, they would get their fill of nourishment. I made sure they were well below the spring, as I had learned my lesson about that in a real personal way.

I built myself a nice fire and prepared my meal. Then I caught myself putting on a pot of coffee. I had told myself back where I supplied up at that I should purchase a coffee pot and plenty of grounds, just in case I had a few visitors. It's my guess that I had myself in mind as the visitor.

I had turned in fairly early, so it was an early rising in the morning. After I had partaken of my meal, I decided that, being I was in no hurry to be anywhere at any time, it just might be interesting to try panning for gold below the spring. That's what I did for the next several hours. I found many small flakes of gold, and a small streak of dust across the crease in the bottom of the pan, but no nuggets at all. I wanted nuggets. The prospector had showed me his nuggets, so consequently I felt that that was all that was important. Being naive in the art of gold prospecting, I picked out all the larger flakes and tossed the rest out on the ground. I rinsed the pan out and returned to the fire. I set the pan on the fire long enough to dry. Then, after it cooled, I packed it away. It was time to move on. I packed up and headed on down the trail.

It was midafternoon when I arrived at a spot where I could see a great distance towards the west. All I could see was desert. I really didn't relish spending the next few days roasting in the hot sun. I left the trail and headed towards the south along the mountain range. I came to a really nice spot just as it was starting to turn dark, so I made a quick camp. After taking care of the horses, I didn't bother eating. I just took a swig of water and turned in without even building a fire. It was peaceful, and sleep came in a hurry.

I must have been more tired than I thought, as it was full daylight when I woke up. I glanced over at the horses and saw that they were still laying down, so I turned over and promptly fell back to sleep.

When my eyes opened again, it was because my belly was growling, telling me that I was starving it. I got up and went about building a fire. I then went to the horses and led them to a small spring that I had spotted downhill from camp. I picketed them below the spring to feed, as there was an abundant amount of grass growing there. Funny how a man learns so fast how much better the water tastes by placing his horses below the water supply. I went back to the fire and made up some bacon, eggs, and a fresh pan of biscuits. The pot of coffee that somehow seemed to become an automatic item in the fire was nearly ready at the same time my meal was. I enjoyed it all.

I was in no hurry to get anywhere, and this was a great place to camp, so I decided to stay for a time. I had no desire to attack that desert any time soon. The air was becoming quite cold, and a night fire was something I needed to make a habit of building before turning in at night. It had been pretty cold the night before, and I had taken one of the horse's saddle blankets and placed that over the top of my wool blanket that covered my body from my neck down. It didn't smell the best, but the warmth was a welcome thing. I would make it a habit each day to bring in a good supply of firewood. I made the decision to spend the day gathering all the firewood that I could easily find, and then keep building on the supply a little each day. By nightfall, I had quite a pile.

Early the next morning, I took out my shovel and pick and headed towards the draw that I had crossed on the way to this camp. It was only a couple of hundred yards away. When I came to the bottom of the draw, I saw that it had a small dry stream of gravel that led on up to a large patch of brush. I picked my way up towards it. I found the brush was thicker than I wanted to penetrate, so I worked my way uphill around it. When I reached the other side of the brush, the gravel bed seemed to slowly disappear. I found no gold above the brush, so I went back down the hill to where I first started. I picked away downhill for a ways, and then headed back to camp carrying several bags of stream ore that looked promising.

After arriving back at camp, I dumped some of the ore into my gold pan and carried it to the spring. After I had panned all the ore out, I had not found enough gold to make it worth my while. Again, I wanted them big nuggets. I spent the rest of the next several weeks picking around in every direction for a place that might prove out. I found none.

I decided that it was time to move on to another location. I thought if I moved more downhill and towards the south, it might prove to be a little warmer, so that's what I did. Each morning I packed up and moved a little more south, working my way down towards that desert. After another week of this, I came to the edge of the desert floor.

I sat in camp all the next day trying to make up my mind as to which direction I wanted to move. I did that for several more days. On the fourth day, I spotted movement out on the desert floor. I took out my spotting scope and looked it over. It appeared to be a burro with packs on it. It was just meandering around, and there didn't seem to be anybody with it. I saddled my horse and mounted up. I sat there wondering if it was a wise idea to stick my nose into someone else's affairs. Curiosity got the best of me, so I spurred my mount towards the burro. When I approached it, I sat and looked around in every direction, trying to spot the owner.

Once again, I took out my spotting scope and scanned towards where the tracks had come from. I saw nothing. I took up the lead rope on the burro and headed back in the direction the burro had come from. It was becoming quite late, and I had it in mind that I needed to get back to camp before dark. As I was about to head back, I figured I would give it one more look over with my scope. Way off to the south and east, I spotted what I thought might be a small patch of greenery. I made up my mind that I would ride there in the morning and check it out. I then headed back to camp, leading the burro. It was dark when we arrived. I led the burro to the spring and let it drink for a short time, and then picketed it a short way off from the horses. It's been noted that horses and burros don't get along to well.

I went back to the fire, stoked it back up, and cooked myself a steak with some taters. I heated two of the pan biscuits to sop up the juices. There was still plenty of coffee left from the morning, so I heated it up as well. While eating and drinking, I wondered what I would find the next day. I hoped that it wouldn't be a dead body. I had to admit that it didn't look good though.

It was getting quite cold, so I stoked up the fire and piled some more wood on it. I cleaned up the dish and fork, and then turned in with that saddle blanket on top again. I would have to find something more permanent before long. It was just getting too danged cold at night.

When morning came, I couldn't wait to get started, so I grabbed some jerky and a couple of pan biscuits and placed them in one of my saddlebags. I then saddled up my horse and mounted up. As I rode out to where I found the burro, I decided that I would continue following the burro tracks instead of going to that patch of greenery. The tracks meandered all around, but always ended up heading south towards that patch of greenery. I wondered.

In the early afternoon, we arrived at the edge of that patch, and I followed the tracks on into the middle and came to where an old prospector was laying in his bedroll next to his fire. I dismounted and went over to the man, kneeled down and spoke, asking him if he could hear me.

I got the surprise of my life when he spoke and asked me to back off very slowly. He had slipped the barrel of his sidearm up against the underside of my chin. I was more than obliged to comply with his wish. As I slowly backed away, he followed with the gun barrel pointing at my head. I told him that he sure picked a hell of a way to treat a man who had found his burro. His eyes lit up as he looked around for his burro. He gruffly asked where it was. I told him that it was in my camp a few miles north of here. He then asked me why in the hell didn't I bring it back to him. I told him that it was because I didn't know where he was. I then told him that I would sure take it kindly if he lowered that cannon before it went off.

He looked at me, and then looked at his sidearm and said that it couldn't have done me no harm, as he had forgotten to light the fuse. He then slowly lowered it. I thanked him and told him the rest of the story, reassuring him that his burro was all right and I would be bringing it back as soon as he let me go. He just waved his sidearm and said for me to go get him. As I rose to leave, I turned to him and asked if he would ride with me back to camp and get it himself. He said he surly would like to, but he didn't think his legs would let him do it. I asked him what was wrong with his legs. He looked long and hard at me, and then slowly slipped the blanket off of his legs. I about fell over.

Both of his legs were swollen to about twice their normal size. On one of them, I saw a large sore that was oozing with infection. As I looked, he showed me the other one, and it was even worse. I asked him what happened. He said he was working his claim when a slab broke loose and cut both of his legs wide open as it slid on down to the ground. He went on to tell me he had been able to still work the claim for another week before it finally put him down a week ago. I asked him why he didn't seek help. He said that he thought it would heal up, and then his burro walked off, leaving him with no way out of here. Now it was too late.

Chapter Seven

I had to make a quick decision. I reached over and slid his sidearm over out of the way. I told him that I was going to lift him onto my horse and get him some help. He told me to just bring him his burro and let them die in peace. I slid my arms under him and lifted him up into my saddle. I took up the reins, and then led my horse out of the greenery. I told him to hang on tight, as I swung myself up onto the back side of the saddle. I spurred my horse on its way back to my camp. Once we were in camp, I slid down, pulled him off into my arms, and sat him down by the fire. Once his burro saw him, it started braying to beat heck. It wouldn't stop. I went over and led the burro back over to the side of his master. He stopped all his noise and just nuzzled up and down on the old man's face.

I stoked up the fire and began a meal for us. I made a fresh pot of coffee. When everything was ready, I handed the old man a plate and took another for myself. I poured coffee for us both. When I handed him the cup, he began shaking. I asked him what was wrong. He said it had been a month since he had had a cup of coffee, and he loved his coffee. His shaking was in anticipation of getting a swig of it in his belly. I laughed and told him that I had better quit drinking the stuff now while I still can. He gave a quick chuckle.

Once our meal was down, I cleaned everything and settled back down near the old man by the fire. He said he felt better, but his legs were throbbing with pain. I told him that I had some a painkiller if he wanted it. He told me that he would even take a bullet right about then.

I went over to my saddlebags and pulled out one of the last two bottles of whisky that I had. I pulled the cork and handed it to him. He took a long hard pull on the bottle. I had to reach over and pull it away from him. He drank a full one-fourth of the bottle. He slowly began to settle back, with a slight smile slipping across his face. The whisky had done its job. He still had about half of a cup of coffee, so I poured in a shot of the whisky. I told him he had better just sip on it. He did.

I asked him if I could have a better look at his legs, and he told me to go ahead. As I looked at them, it began to make me sick to the stomach. He had gangrene that had advanced to the point that even cutting his legs off wouldn't save him. I told him what I saw. He

Vanishing Anger

told me to take him over to the gully and leave him with a sidearm.

I told him that I had a poultice that I would like to try on it first. I promised him that if that didn't work that I would grant him his wish. He just said to get it done and over with. I went to my bag and pulled out the bag of poultice ingredients. I went back by his side and told him that what I was about to do would hurt him like hell was on fire. He again said to get her done. I pulled out my long blade and stuck it in the fire. When it was red hot, I handed him the bottle and let him take a large swig of it. I then withdrew the knife from the fire and placed the blade on the wound, sliding the knife over the opening. Everywhere the knife touched the flesh sizzled. He was screaming all kinds of bloody murder. I then spread some of poultice medicine over the wound and wrapped a rag around it.

I stuck the knife back in the fire. When he saw that, he screamed again, asking if I was going to do that with the other leg. I nodded my head yes. He told me that he would need two good pulls of that whisky for that one. I told him he had earned it. I gave him the bottle, he took a long swig, and then after a few seconds took another. With that, he had finished just over half of that bottle of whisky. I took the bottle and set it down out of his reach. I reached over, withdrew the knife from the fire, and commenced to do the same to that wound as I did to his other leg. He screamed out that I was a sadistic bastard, and then passed out.

I put the knife back in the fire, waited for it to turn red, and then once again took it and carved large chunks of rotting meat from his legs. When I was done, I seared the wounds closed, recoated both legs with the poultice, and wrapped them both in cloth rags.

My only hope now was that the poison that was spreading up his legs would reverse itself. The old prospector didn't wake up for several hours. When he did, I handed him a cup of coffee laced with a shot of whisky. He gulped it down and handed the cup back, asking for more. I refilled his cup, only put in a half of a shot, and then handed it back. I told him to sip it, as it was the last he would get tonight. He did. When he had finished, he once again slipped off into a sound sleep. I was glad. I covered him up with my blanket and the saddle blanket. I then went over, pulled out the other saddle blanket, and sat down near the prospector. I had moved my saddle over by him. I laid back against it, covered myself the best I could, and fell soundly asleep.

Vanishing Anger

When I woke up it was just breaking dawn. I looked over at the old prospector and saw he was still asleep. I looked over at the horses; they appeared to be all right. I got up and stoked the fire back up. I then went over and took care of the horses. It didn't take much, as they had been picketed in reach of water, and there was plenty of feed all around them. I walked back to the fire, and I heard the old prospector groaning. I couldn't think of anything I could do to relieve his pain, so I went back to putting together a meal. I placed coffee on the fire first, and then began cooking up some venison steaks. I used up the last of the eggs to make up a batch of hotcakes. When the coffee was ready, I poured a cup for the old prospector and went by his side to hand it to him. As I reached the cup toward him, he grabbed my arm and had a wild look in his eyes.

He struggled to speak. Finally, he whispered, telling me to look on the underside of his burro's pack frame. I rose, walked over to the pack frame, and rolled it over. Tucked under one of the wide belly straps was a piece of worn-out leather. That was all I saw that looked out of place. I tugged at it a few times and it eventually slipped out. When I took it back over to the prospector's side, I asked him if that was what he wanted. He nodded his head yes. I went to hand it to him, but he shook his head and whispered for me to spread it open. I did as he asked. Inside of the piece of leather was a map with an X marked on it. It had directions as to how to find it.

He whispered, "Gold!" His eyes got really big. He again whispered that the gold was very large nuggets and the pool was full of them.

He was really struggling to talk. I didn't say a word. I just let him try. The last words he whispered before he slipped off to his death were, "It's all yours!"

I threw the map down next to my saddle, picked up my shovel, and went over on a small knoll and dug a grave as deep as the rocks would let me, which was only a couple of feet. I picked his body up, carried it over to the shallow grave, and gently placed it in the bottom. I then placed a mound of dirt over the grave, and then gathered a lot of rocks and stacked them all over and around the grave, to keep the animals from digging him up. I fashioned out a cross, tying it together with leather strips. I flattened one side of the cross arm and wrote on it, "Here lies an old prospector."

I went back by the fire, finished my breakfast, and then sat down to a cup of coffee.

Vanishing Anger

As I sat there, I thought, *Damn! I sure didn't want that old prospector to die.* I had done all I could and shouldn't have any regrets, but I did. I finished my coffee, and then went over and prepared the animals for moving on.

After placing the last pack frame on the burro and had finished loading all my gear, I walked the animals over to the old prospector's grave and stood there for a moment. I mounted up and started to head for his campsite to look around to see what more I could find out about the old man. As I rode by the dead campfire, I spotted the piece of leather with the map on it. I dismounted, retrieved the map, and then remounted and left for his camp.

I arrived at his camp just after high noon. I set camp. The old prospector had enough firewood stacked around the place to last several winters. As I was staking the animals over near the spring, I noticed something sticking out from under some of the brush. I reached over, pulled it out, and saw that it was one of the old prospector's pack sacks. When I opened it, I found two leather pouches inside. One of the pouches was about a third of the way full of gold nuggets, all about the size of one of my small fingernails. I opened the other pouch and found it about one quarter of the way full of gold dust and flakes. I looked for the other pack sack and found it near his bedroll. There was nothing in it. All his food was hanging from the branch of a small tree back under the cover of its green foliage. Now all I had to do was find the gold's source.

After unpacking all of my supplies, I went through all of the old prospector's personal belongings to see if I could find anything identifying next of kin. I found none. I did find some papers showing that he had acquaintances in England. There were no addresses. I sat there looking at everything. Finally, I just accepted the fact that I was now the new owner. I decided to sort it all out, burn everything that I didn't need, and clean and use all the items I could. It had become late, so I made a fire and cooked some steaks and taters. When I was done eating, I turned in for the night. It had been a long, sad day. I really had wanted that old prospector to live. It was a fitful night, but sleep did eventually overcome me.

When morning came, breakfast was consumed, and I had taken care of the animals, I decided to study that leather map. It spoke of the last place the sun shone on the mountain. On the part where it said the gold was located where the X was marked, the map had a tear that almost came loose. I figured that the only

Vanishing Anger

way I would understand it was to watch the sun set on the mountain. After finishing going through the old prospector's stuff, I went around to the east side of the greenery and studied the mountain range before me. That didn't do me any good.

While sitting there, I noticed a set of tracks that led towards the mountain. The more I looked the area over, I found many more sets of tracks, which included human ones, leading back and forth to and from that mountain. I got up and went back inside the patch of greenery. I saddled up my horse, mounted up, and followed those tracks all the way to a very steep canyon with shear walls on both sides. The tracks led me on into that canyon. I finally reached a spot that had an opening in the bottom of the draw that was before me. I dismounted and tied my horse off to a bush. I followed the tracks to that opening. It turned out to be pretty large, and I could hear water running in it.

As I entered the opening, I could hear the water more clearly, but it was back into the cave far enough that it was dark and I couldn't see anything. It sounded like a small waterfall. I thought there must be a pool at its base. I headed back out and made my way back to camp. When I reached it, the day was pretty much over, so I decided to wait until the next morning to investigate the cave further. I stripped the saddle from my horse and took care of the animals.

After a while, it began turning to dusk, so I built up a fire and prepared my meal. The old prospector had an oil lamp, so I lit it. It was pretty bright for an oil lamp. I checked around and found a jar of oil. It was over half full. It must have been about a gallon-sized jar. I wondered where he'd gotten his lamp oil and supplies. When I was done eating, I turned down the lantern and slid into my bedroll for the night. Sleep again was spotty. That damned gold stuff had me hooked.

Chapter Eight

When morning came, it was earlier than I wanted. I didn't start a fire. I picked out some jerky and pan biscuits, along with some water, and then placed it all on the burro with all my prospecting tools. I went over and checked to make sure my horses were all right. Once satisfied all was secure, I led the burro out of the patch of greenery and headed straight for that cave. It took me a little longer, but at least I wouldn't have to worry about the horses while I was gone.

When I arrived at the mouth of the canyon, I had to navigate my way through all the boulders that had fallen from the cliff sides. The old prospector had cleared a path through the obstructions. I arrived at the opening of the cave that was located a few feet above the valley floor. My burro could go no farther. I secured the animal and off loaded its packboards.

I was now ready to explore that cave. I took up the lantern, lit it, and then made my way to the entrance. As I entered, I had a strange feeling come over me. I shook it off and made my way on into the cave. Once again that strange feeling came over me. I couldn't figure out what it was. I again shook it off and continued on in farther. There it was, a large pool with a waterfall that fed it. I noticed that the water filtered its way on out through the rocks and disappeared near the entrance to the cave. I figured it must be the source of the spring at my camp. Everything I saw excited me. It was so perfect. Again, that strange feeling came over me. It was starting to bother me. I tried shaking it off to no avail. It was an eerie feeling.

I went ahead and continued my quest to see if this was indeed the source of the old prospector's gold. I shoveled a load of gravel into my gold pan and commenced to pan it out. I was astonished with what I saw, without even finishing. There were small nuggets throughout the gravel. As I was picking them out, I found three larger nuggets. I now knew that this was the source of the old prospectors' gold. I filled several small bags with the gravel. After tying them shut, I packed everything up and headed back out of the cave. When I reached the mouth of the cave, that strange feeling came over me again. I thought, *What the hell is that?*

I placed the pack back on the burro and loaded all my gear and the bags of gravel on it.

Vanishing Anger

I led the burro out through the labyrinth of boulders. Once out of the canyon, I headed straight for camp. A sense of urgency came over me. I pushed hard until I reached the patch of greenery. I worked my way around to the opening and got the shock of my life. There was blood spattered everywhere. Both of my horses were gone. I followed the blood trail out into the desert. I spotted one of my horses laying off in the distance. When I arrived by its side, I found it dead. Parts of it had been eaten away. It was the horse that I rode. Tears came to my eyes. I hadn't realized that I even had emotions other than anger.

Once the shock had worn off, I began looking for signs of the packhorse. When I arrived at the entrance to the patch of greenery, I spotted the tracks of my packhorse heading straight west into the desert. I began following the tracks. It was not until five or six miles out that I found the animal and saw that it was in dire shape. Most of the rear quarter on one side had been torn to shreds. I could tell that there was no way it could survive. I reluctantly withdrew my .44 and put the animal out of its misery. As I stood there, the thought of my burro being unprotected back in camp came over me. I began running towards camp in a panic. The sun was scorching hot, and I stumbled and fell a number of times. I had to make it back to camp.

As I neared the opening into the patch of greenery, I spotted a cougar off in the distance walking my way. It evidently had not spotted me yet, as it was continuing its way towards my camp. I slipped off to one side and tucked myself into the edge of the foliage. I could see the cougar advancing as I sat there motionless. I withdrew my .44 once again. I cocked the hammer back in anger. It made a noise, and the cougar stopped and studied the source of it. It angered me that I had been so careless. The cougar evidently felt that it might be the other horse, so it crouched down and slowly and cautiously advanced towards the opening.

When it reached to a distance of about thirty feet, it suddenly stopped and began sniffing the air. It had sensed danger and was spinning around to run away. I jumped out and emptied my sidearm at it. The last shot hit it, and it stumbled and fell. While I was running towards the cougar, I was struggling but accomplished reloading my .44. As I neared the cougar, it began showing its teeth and snarling at me. It was just beginning to regain its footing when I again unloaded my pistol into it. This time it was down for good. I stood over it with much anger in my heart. I reloaded my weapon and once again emptied it into the cougar. It was already dead, but I had to get rid of my pent-up anger somewhere.

I then kicked the cougar a dozen or more times. I finally wore out and headed back to my camp to check on the burro. It was terrified, but appeared to be unharmed. I took out some grain and hand fed it to the burro. I whispered into its ear as I fed it, and it started to calm down. After a few minutes, the wild look in its eyes began to fade away. I couldn't afford to lose this animal. It and I were going to become good pals. Once I was sure the animal had calmed down, I began checking it over for any injuries. I found none. The cougar must not have made it back to the camp. I was relieved.

My stomach began telling me that I had not eaten since yesterday. I hadn't eaten any of the biscuits or jerky while gathering the gravel from the pool. It had been too exciting of a time to think about my belly. Then it hit me—all of what was happening here in camp was what those feelings of uneasiness were about. It then came to mind that if I had dropped everything when I first had those feelings and came back to camp I may have been able to save my horses. That thought angered me beyond what I could stand. I began screaming at myself, running around, and once again firing my .44 at everything out in the desert. I tired and fell to the ground totally exhausted. It was the angriest I had ever been in my life.

The hot sun was beating down on me. I had to get back to where there was some shade. I struggled to get up and ended up crawling back into camp. I hit my bedroll and passed out. I woke up to the burro braying. I grabbed for my .44 and found it wasn't there. The burro quieted down. I shakily got up, went over to the burro, and once again held out a handful of grain. Again, I whispered into its ear as it ate. It seemed to be content. I knew that I must not ever let that burro out of my sight again. It would now be my closest companion. It evidently felt my compassion for it, because it swung its head over to my face and gently began nuzzling it. That was the same thing it had done to the old prospector.

All of a sudden, those hunger pangs hit me with a vengeance. I went over, grabbed up a biscuit, stuffed the whole thing into my mouth, and washed it down with water. I then reached over and found a piece of jerky and did likewise. Once I had it washed down, I grabbed up another biscuit and began cramming it into my mouth. When it was consumed, I washed it down with water again.

I sat down hard. I tumbled back onto my bedroll and once again fell asleep.

I awoke several hours later, feeling worn out all over. I decided that I would take the next several days off and recuperate. No part of my body wanted to move. All of a sudden, a calmness came over me. It was a peacefulness that I had not felt before. All my pent-up anger seemed to melt away. I guessed the man upstairs felt that I had had enough and emptied me of all the bitterness and anger that always seemed to haunt me. I even sat there with a smile on my face. I didn't know what had happened, but it sure felt good. The thought came to mind that the burro must have felt that I went loco. I don't know. Maybe I did, but I liked the feeling.

I began whistling as I made up a fire and prepared my meal. I made a fresh pot of coffee and placed that on the fire. As I finished my meal, the coffee told me that it was ready. I poured a cup and began drinking it. After a couple of swallows, I thought, *Damn that's good stuff!* Again I looked at the cup and said to myself, "What the hell happened to me? I hated this damned coffee before."

I chuckled as I cleaned everything up. When I was done, I decided that I had better see if I could find out what had happened to my sidearm. When I couldn't find it around camp, I walked outside and looked around. I spotted it a short way away, so I went and retrieved it. Once back in camp, I cleaned my .44 and reloaded it. I then re-holstered it. I noticed that my belt was almost devoid of bullets, so I went over to my pack and reloaded all the loops. I reached over to my other pack and pulled out my spare .44. I checked it out as well and decided to clean it. I reloaded it, and then stuffed it back into the pack. I went over to my saddle, removed my .44-40, and cleaned and reloaded it. I pulled out the shotgun and cleaned it as well.

As I sat there looking around, the thought came to me that I wouldn't be needing that saddle again for a while. I would take it with me when I walked for supplies. I thought, *Walked! Hell, I haven't walked anywhere since I left the shipping piers.* That was a rude awakening. It now dawned on me that I had better check everything over and make a list of everything I needed to sustain myself. I would need to look for a new mount when I went to Beatty. The thought of having to walk all the way there didn't seem to bother me. Before it would have angered me till all hell broke loose.

Vanishing Anger

I thought, *What the hell has happened to me? I've become a whole new person.*

As I sat there, I decided that I would leave in the morning for Beatty. I ate a bite and turned in for the night.

Chapter Nine

When morning came, I stoked up the fire, and then made some pan biscuits. I fried up a steak and a few potatoes that were left. When I had finished eating and had everything cleaned up, I placed the packboards on the burro. The burro must have sensed that we were heading out on a long trip, as it began nuzzling up and down on my face, and then started braying. I emptied everything out of the pack sacks. The only thing I placed in them was enough food to get me to Beatty. I figured that if I moved steady I could make it in two or three days. I took my gold and buried it in the ground under some branches. I didn't need any of it, as I still had quite a bit of money from the sale of the horses along with their saddles. I had also sold the gold that the prospector that I killed had. The money should last for a few trips.

When I was sure everything was secure in camp, I took the lead rope and began my journey to Beatty. It took me most of the day to make it to where I had buried the old prospector. When I arrived, the burro started braying and tugging on the rope, telling me it wanted to visit its old owner. I relented and walked over to the grave. When we were at the gravesite, the burro began braying over and over. I just stood off to the side and let it get it out of its system. It finally quit, and then looked at me with a forlorn look. I spoke quietly to the burro for a minute or so. It moved closer to my side, and then nuzzled my face. I asked it if it was ready to go. It nuzzled my face again, so I took it as a yes. I began walking towards where the trail was located. It was dark when I arrived.

I set camp for the night, built a small fire, and then cooked my meal. I had the coffee on, so after I ate my meal, I poured myself a cup. It was mighty good. I thought to myself, *When in hell did I start thinking that about coffee?* I was really hooked on the stuff now. I drank more than half of the pot before I quit for the night.

I cleaned up my cooking gear and went over and checked on the burro. It was in a nice patch of green grass and had enough water within reach. I left enough loose rope for it to be comfortable. I went to my bedroll and turned in for the night. Sleep came fast. It was a sound sleep.

I woke up to the burro braying again. It was just beginning to turn daylight. I supposed this was how it was going to be from then on.

It was going to be my alarm clock. I got up and stoked the fire back to life. I then went over and checked the burro. Once I was sure all was well, I returned to the fire and cooked myself a steak. When the coffee was done, I had just finished my steak. I poured myself a cup and relaxed with my back leaning up against the saddle. Once I had all I wanted of the coffee, I poured the remainder over the fire and began cleaning up all my cooking gear. I had just completed placing everything back on the burro when I spotted a rider coming down the trail. I walked over to the side of the trail to let the horse and rider pass. As the rider passed, he stared long and hard at my burro. He stopped then rode back to me.

Once he was stopped in front of me, he asked where I got the burro. I told him that an old prospector had walked up to me while I was heading back to my camp and was leading this burro. I saw that he had some severe injuries. I told him that the old prospector had collapsed right in front of me, and that I loaded him on my horse and took him and his burro back to my camp. His wounds were too far gone, and the old prospector died from gangrene and blood poisoning. I said that I had done everything I knew how to do for him, but it wasn't enough. The old prospector

Vanishing Anger

had asked me to take his burro and treat it right if he didn't survive. I left it at that. Most of what I said was true. The rider said he was sorry to hear that, as he had liked the old prospector.

I asked the rider if he knew where the old prospector's camp was. He told me that nobody had ever been able to find out. He said the old prospector was a pretty wily old bird. He always mislead those that tried to follow him. Everybody seemed to think his mine was somewhere near the ridge north of the trail. I told the rider that I was coming from the west when he had stumbled onto me, and the old prospector said that he got hurt in his mine and had stumbled his way down trying to make it to Lone Pine to get help. I said that I had buried the old prospector good and proper near my camp. I also told him that I had searched through his packs and found no gold or anything that would identify any relatives.

The rider said that it was a shame that he hadn't told me where his mine was, because he was getting some nice nuggets out of it. He was watching for some sign on my face that I knew the location. I remained pretty poker-faced. I was always pretty good at that. I told the rider that I had better get moving, as I had to make Beatty to supply up. He asked me if I had a horse. I told him that a cougar had jumped my horses while I was prospecting and killed both of them. He said that that explained the saddle draped over the pack frame. I just said "yep" and moved on.

I rode just over the crest, and then doubled back up onto a small knoll and looked back on the trail. I had a bad feeling about that rider.

I saw nobody, so I continued down the trail towards Beatty. It was well after dark when I arrived. I made camp just short of the settlement. I turned in after consuming a couple of pan biscuits and some jerky. I'd have coffee in the morning at the eatery in Beatty.

I was woken up early when the burro sounded the alarm. I packed up and made my way into the settlement. The eatery was just opening. I tied off the burro and went in to have breakfast and coffee. When that was done, I made my way over to the blacksmith shop. I asked the man to check my burro out to see if it needed shoes. He lifted each leg, and then turned to me and said they were just fine. He asked me where I got the burro, so I had to tell the whole story all over again. He said it was a shame, as he had really liked the old prospector.

I offered to pay, but he just said I didn't owe anything. I thanked him. I asked him if he knew of any horses for sale, and he lit up and said he sure wished he did, as he would buy it himself. I told him yes, and that he would then make a healthy profit off of me. He said that was pretty much how it went around there. There was a pretty severe shortage of horses around that part of the country. He asked me if I wanted to sell the saddle, and I said I might just as well, as I didn't have a horse to put it on. He offered me fifty dollars for it, and I said that it wasn't near enough. I started to leave, when he yelled for me to hold up a minute. He then offered me a hundred for it and I accepted. He offloaded the saddle before I could change my mind. I thanked him again and left for the mercantile.

When I reached the mercantile, I tied the burro off at the hitch rail and went inside to purchase all my needed supplies. I bought extra of everything. The burro would have its work cut out for it, as the load would be heavy. When I finished getting my supplies, I headed for the door, with the old man carrying a bag for me, as I had purchased so much. I stopped short of the door after spotting that same rider across the way, standing there watching my burro. I asked the owner if he recognized the man. He said he did. He told me to watch my back around that one. I told the owner to set my bag down by the door and not to look at the man. He did as I asked. I didn't look up as I carried the sacks over to the burro and loaded them into the packsacks. I went back in, picked up the last sack, and turned for the door again. I saw the man still standing there. I nonchalantly loaded the last sack into the packs.

I unhitched the burro and led it towards the eatery. I tied the burro off and went inside. I sat where I could still see the man standing across the way. He seemed to be pretty impatient. It was still early, but I ate a large meal anyway. I didn't want to stop until it was well after dark once I was back on the trail.

I paid up and began my trek towards the trail. I started up the trail and it became dark as I was walking along. There was just enough moonlight that I could still see my way. I walked my way on up to just before I reached the crest. I then veered off the trail towards the north. I had traveled several hundred yards, when I turned back down the mountain another couple of hundred yards. I set up on a spot that overlooked the trail. I tied the burro off to some brush down out of sight, and then tucked myself in so as not to be seen.

I fell asleep. Just before sunup, the burro began braying. I jumped up, ran over to the

Vanishing Anger

burro, and silenced it. I then tied the burro off to where it could see me, and then went back to where I had fallen asleep. I didn't want to do that again. I waited for another hour or so, when sure as hell that same rider came along. He was looking down, watching for my tracks. I retrieved the burro, doubled back down, and fell in several hundred yards behind the rider. I walked up the trail until I finally spotted the man. He was looking up off to the side of the trail. I hid the burro and myself, and then watched the man as he worked his way north of the trail, following my tracks. When he had disappeared out of sight, I began back up the trail once again. When I crested the mountain, I again turned off the trail and headed north for a ways. I turned back towards the crest, and when I reached it, I sat and watched my back trail. Sure enough, an hour later there he was, heading up the trail watching for my tracks.

I turned north, and when I spotted a long rock slab that must have been several hundred yards long, I walked to it. When I had walked on it several hundred feet, I turned back towards the trail. When I reached the edge of the slab, I stopped and cut off a real brushy branch. As I walked downhill, I would tie off the burro and walk back to wipe out all of our tracks. I did that for a long way.

I had worked our way to south of the trail several hundred yards and we entered some thick brush. I went back and finished wiping out the last of our tracks. I sat there waiting for several hours. As I did, I heard hoofbeats coming down the trail. They were faint, as the trail was quite a distance from me. Pretty soon I could see the rider coming down the trail looking for tracks. He rode on down out of sight. I didn't move, as I was sure that he would be riding back this way.

It was several hours before he showed back up. He was riding along on the side of the trail a short distance from me. I slid back under the brush a little farther. He was too close for comfort. I drew my .44 out of its holster and had my thumb on the hammer, waiting to see if I would need it. He rode past me within about fifteen feet. Why he didn't see me or sense my presence I don't know. He passed me heading uphill and was beginning to work his way back towards the trail. Once he was back on the trail, he stopped and looked around in every direction. He was ranting about something, but I couldn't make out what he was saying. I'd bet my gold that it wasn't anything very nice. After he rode up the trail

Vanishing Anger

out of sight, I went around the brush, took hold of the burro's lead rope, and headed downhill for my new desert home. I stayed off and away from the trail.

Chapter Ten

I made camp early, as both the burro and I were exhausted. We would reach our desert camp about noon tomorrow if nothing interrupted us on the way. I knew we both would welcome that. I ate jerky, along with pan biscuits, and drank water. I wanted no fire. I took my hat, poured quite a bit of the remaining water in it, and sat it down by the burro. It drank long and hard. After I had removed the pack from its back, I watched as the burro slowly relax from the overburdened load. I made up my mind that I would not do that again after this trip. I even contemplated leaving some of the load there and returning for it later. I thought I had better not do that, as bear would strip everything to shreds. The burro would just have to bear the load another half of a day.

After a good night's sleep, I loaded the pack back on the burro and wasted no time heading on towards our camp. We arrived about an hour before noon. As I didn't want any more surprises, we entered the camp warily. Everything was in good shape. I offloaded the burro, and after picketing it near the spring where it could drink and feed its little old heart out, I began sorting all of my supplies. I must have thought I was going to open up a mercantile, as I had so many supplies. I had enough food to last for several months. Nearly all of it was canned jars full of one thing or another. How none of it broke, I will never know. I was glad I had it. I made up a fire, and then put a pot of coffee on. I wanted that pretty bad. I was really hooked on that stuff.

When the coffee was done, I poured myself a cup and took out a biscuit and some jerky. I chewed on the jerky, took a bite of the biscuit, and then sipped on the coffee. For some reason, it all tasted like a gourmet meal. I savored it. I shook out my bedroll and laid back on it, using one of the pack sacks as a pillow. It had a couple of blankets in it, so it was quite comfortable. After a short time, I sat back up and poured myself another cup of that delicious coffee. I sat there sipping on coffee and planning my next move. I decided that I would head over to the cave in the morning and pan out as much gold as I could before dark.

After a while, I thought about that cougar laying out there. I went out with the shovel and buried its carcass. Thoughts of the horses went through my mind, and it saddened me. I tried to shake it out of my mind, but it lingered on for a time.

I got up, dug out my telescope, and then went outside of the patch of greenery. I began walking around the perimeter of my camp. As I did, I stopped every few yards and scoped out the horizon to see if there was anything moving around out there. I spotted a few vultures in the area of the horse carcasses. Again, it saddened me. I moved on each time. After completely navigating my way around the patch of greenery and was satisfied that there was nothing lurking, I returned to my camp for the night.

I cooked a steak, and some potatoes with carrots mixed in with them. It made for a good meal. It was the last piece of meat I had, so I would have to go find another deer sometime in the next few days. They were plentiful up on the mountainside. I drank the last of the coffee, and then checked on the burro to see if it was doing all right. It was, so I turned in for the night.

When morning came, I was in no hurry to get up. I had to briefly get up to stifle the burro's braying wake-up call. I crawled back into my bedroll and fell right back to sleep. The sun was full up when I woke again. I must have needed the sleep, and I felt no need to begrudge myself of it. Time was all mine now, and I could do whatever I wanted any time I wanted. I had no timeline for anything. I was getting mentally cocky about it. I laughed at the thought. I got up and started the fire again. I put the coffee on, and then dug out some eggs and made pancakes. I found the syrup and poured it over them. It was good. After cleaning everything up and putting it away, I went over to the burro and placed the packboards back on it. I loaded my mining supplies, along with the lantern, and headed for the mine.

It was close to noon before I reached my destination. I was in no hurry. Life was good. I tied the burro off to some brush, and then offloaded the packboards. I took up my gold pan and shovel and brought the lantern with me as well. I climbed up and into the cave. I lit the lamp and set it on a ledge near the pool. I panned out gold until I could see the sun was beginning to set. It was hard to quit, as I had found one large nugget and wanted another. I was being greedy. I picked up the pan and shovel, reached up and took down the lantern, and then headed out of the cave. When I exited the cave, I turned off the lantern. I loaded everything back onto the burro and headed back to camp.

It was just turning dark when I arrived. I took care of the burro, and then started a fire. I put on coffee. I opened a jar of stew and heated it up. It was really tasty. The coffee hit the spot as well. I turned in for the night.

As dawn broke through the darkness of the night, I woke up. My alarm clock had gone off. I got up, went over to my burro, and shut its alarm off by whispering in its ear. That always seemed to do the trick. The burro had taken up the habit of nuzzling up and down on my face after I was done whispering. It and I seemed to have really jelled together since we visited its old master's gravesite. It had been my constant companion since I buried the old prospector. Every time I spoke, it was to that burro or another presence, though I still didn't understood what that was. I hadn't stoked up a fire as of yet, but felt a need to take up my scope and go outside of the patch of greenery to check things out. As I walked around the outskirts of my camp, I stopped every few steps and scoped in every direction.

When I had reached the north side of my camp, I spotted movement far off in the distance. I slipped back under the brush to conceal myself and watch. It seemed to be getting closer and closer. Finally, I could see that it was a horse and rider, and could tell that they were heading straight towards my camp. They were still a long distance away. I slowly slipped my way back into camp and loaded all my gear back on the burro. There was a slight opening in the greenery that was on the south side of the camp, so we slipped out through it and walked quite a distance towards the south. I walked west another long distance, and then walked north until I could see the rider again. I walked farther to a point where I was due west of the rider.

I took up the scope again and studied the rider once more. As I looked, it hit me with a thud! *It's that damned man that was trying to follow me to my mine.* I now had to conger up a plan as to how I was going to detour him. I withdrew my .44 and fired a shot in the air. It stopped the man dead in his tracks. I could tell he was studying me. I holstered my .44 and began walking towards him. He also made the decision to make his way towards me. The time was flying by. When he had ridden up to within ten yards or so, he stopped. I didn't mince words. I came right out and asked him why he was following me. He didn't mince words either. He spat out that he wanted my gold and the mine it came from.

We looked at each other for quite some time, waiting for one or the other to make the next move. He had his horse facing me head on. I suspected it was to protect him from my shooting him. When I saw him go for his sidearm, I instinctively dove to where the horse's head was between him and me. He evidently didn't think about that possibility, as he just swung his sidearm to follow me and fired. He shot his horse in the back of the head. When his horse went down and he was flailing the air to catch himself, I withdrew my sidearm and pounced on him. I was about to put a bullet in his head, when the thought came to mind that he was now pretty harmless. I looked at him and told him to get up. I reached over, removed his rope lasso from his saddle, and tied him up. I took the loose end and tied it to the back of my burro's pack frame.

I led him away from my camp in a northwesterly direction. After a couple of hours, I turned southwest and walked another couple of hours. I stopped and walked over to him. I looked him in the eyes and told him that it was going to be a long, slow, self-inflicted death for him. He asked me what I was going to do. I said that he and I were going to sit there and have a few drinks together. The bottle of Irish whisky was still in the packsacks. I had left my water pouch on the pack as well. I withdrew them and walked back over to the man. I pulled the cork, held the bottle to his lips, and made him take a long drink. I then took up the water pouch and took a swig of water. I told him that I would drink with him, except I had never taken up the habit. I gave him another long swig of the whisky. He was now drinking more freely.

After he had consumed about half of the bottle, I placed the cork back in it and sat it down in the hot sand. It was a scorcher out here. I went around behind him and removed the rope from around him. I went over to my burro and placed the water pouch back in the pack. He asked me what I was going to do with him now. I just smiled and said that I was going to forgive him and set him free. He had a big grin and thanked me. I started leading the burro in a northeast direction. He yelled over to me to wait for him. I just smiled and told him that I was in a hurry to get to Beatty and sell all the gold that I had.

After an hour or so, I turned in the direction of Lone Pine. It was late in the day when I arrived. I wasted no time in resupplying and heading towards my camp. I made camp a short distance to the southwest of town. In the morning, I swung a little south, following my old tracks to see if the man was still on his feet.

After about four hours, I spotted him. It took another hour to reach him. He was sitting on his legs and looking up at me. While looking up, he asked why I was walking back this way. I told him that I had gone in the wrong direction, and when I finally had it figured out as to which direction I was supposed to go, I headed back. I told him that I sure as heck didn't want to lead him on a wild goose chase following my tracks. I told him that a man could die out here in the middle of the desert. I took out my water pouch and took a drink. I spotted the bottle laying a few yards away, empty. I could tell he was wasted. I picked up the lead rope and began my walk towards my camp. He screamed for me not to leave him. I just yelled back, telling him to follow my tracks, and when he made it to my camp, I would have plenty of water and food waiting for him. I never stopped. I trekked on towards camp and arrived in the dark of night.

I picked up the lantern and relit it. Everything seemed to be in place. I removed the gear from the burro and took care of it by tethering it near the pool where there was plenty of feed. It had been a hard trek for it, just as it had been for me. I gave it a bait of grain, and then went over and rebuilt the fire. Once that was going good, I took out two biscuits and a couple of pieces of jerky and found there was a little coffee still in the pot, so I washed it all down with that. Damn, that coffee was strong! I crawled over and slipped into my bedroll. I then turned the lamp off and promptly fell asleep.

Something woke me in the middle of the night. There was still plenty of moonlight to see by. My first thought was a cougar, but thought better of that, as the burro would have been acting up. After seeing nothing out of place, I slipped back into my bedroll and promptly fell back to sleep.

Chapter Eleven

I had slept late. The last several weeks had been quite tiring. I felt well rested as I rose from my bedroll. I checked the burro, and then walked outside of the patch of greenery, as I always did each morning. I was almost back to the entryway when I spotted a dark spot way off in the distance. I had failed to bring my scope with me, so I went back to the pouch and retrieved it. I strapped on my .44 and went back towards where I had seen that dark spot. I thought sure it must be another cougar; perhaps the mate to the one I killed. I lifted the scope and studied the dark spot for quite some time. It looked like it was slithering low to the sand so as not to be spotted by me. I made up my mind that I had to investigate and take care of the matter before it became a problem.

I placed the scope back in the pouch, and then threw a water pouch over my shoulder and began walking towards where that dark spot was. It took the better part of an hour to reach before I could make out what it was. I was shocked when I saw it was the man that I had left a great distance away out in the desert.

I began slowly walking towards him. I couldn't believe it. He was barely still alive. I thought about having mercy and putting a bullet in his head, but decided to let him live. He was trying to talk to me. His voice was barely audible, as his mouth and throat was so parched from the desert heat and lack of water. He was asking me to help him. I just stood there looking down on him.

After a moment of staring at him, I asked him if his days of thievery were over and he nodded his head yes. I told him that if he made it into my camp I would nurse him back to good health and take him to safety. I took the water pouch from my shoulder and took a good long drink, making sure that I was spilling a great deal of it onto the sand where he could see it. He began trying to work his way to where the water was dripping. I began walking towards camp, while pouring water over the top of my head. He was begging me to stop. I did. I looked him right in the eyes and said that I was a man of my word, and if he by some miracle did make it to my camp I would do just as I had told him I would.

With determination, he began crawling towards me as I turned to continue my walk back to camp. Every so often, I turned and looked back, and each time I witnessed him struggling to make it. Finally, I just left him behind and headed back to camp at a fast pace. I was hungry. When I reached my camp, I looked back out to where the man was and saw that he was still struggling along. I figured he might just give up pretty soon and die. I built my fire back up and began laying out all that I needed for breakfast. I had decided on pancakes and eggs. I had the coffee boiling while dishing up my plate. The pancakes were mighty good, with all that maple syrup that I had poured over them. When the eggs and pancakes had been consumed, I poured myself a cup of coffee, sat back against that pack that I had been using for a pillow, and enjoyed several cups of the stuff.

After I had everything cleaned up and put away, I felt tired again, so I went back to my bedroll. I had no more than laid down when I fell asleep. Several hours later I awoke. I sat up and looked around. I really was out. I must have needed the extra sleep. I figured that I wouldn't get much mining done that day, so I decided to take the burro for a walk around camp to keep it loosened up. I untied its picket, took up its lead rope, and headed for the entrance. Just as I was about to exit, I got the shock of my life. About ten yards out from camp laid the man. He appeared to be dead, so

I went back and retrieved my shovel to give the man a decent burial. I felt that was the least I could do for him.

As I began to exit the camp again, the man moaned. I couldn't believe he was still alive. I walked over to him and looked down. All I said was that, as I had told him, I was a man of my word. I said that I would do my best to get him back on his feet and delivered to a place where he could find a new career. I threw the shovel back towards the entrance of camp, then reached down, grabbed his wrists, and dragged him near the fire. I walked over, took up one of the horse blankets that I had kept, laid it out on the ground, and rolled him over onto it. I walked over, picked up my water pouch, placed the opening against his lips, and told him to only drink a little at a time until he became better able to handle it. He just nodded his head. I let him have two swallows and placed the bag down out of his reach.

I went over to where I had some leftover pancake mix and began cooking up one, along with an egg. I knew I would have to get some food into him if he was going to have a chance to survive. When it was ready, I soaked the pancake in some sugar syrup to make it soft. I knew that it had to be plenty soft before he would be able to swallow it. I placed a very small piece of pancake on my fork and slipped it into his mouth. I told him to not bother trying to chew it, but just swallow, as it was soaked to where it was almost a mushy texture. He swallowed and then gagged on it until it finally went down. I then gave him a sip of water. I continued that process until he had consumed the entire pancake and the egg. I then told him to just relax and try getting some sleep. He went out like a lantern.

He woke up, asking in a raspy voice for some more water. I asked him if he thought he would like some coffee, and he nodded his head yes. I first gave him a swallow of water, and then, after setting the pouch well out of his reach, I went back over by the fire and poured him a half of a cup of the coffee. I let it sit for some time to cool down so it wouldn't burn his throat. I then held it to his lips and let him sip as he was able. He drank it all, and then thanked me for it. I told him that I didn't understand what the hell had come over me, wanting to help a scoundrel like him. I said that I should have just shot him out in the desert and left him for the vultures. He whispered that he surely deserved it. That took me back a little. I said no more.

It took three days before he was strong enough to where he could sit up on his own.

Each night I tied his wrists up, and then tied the other end to a tree over on the opposite side of the fire from me. I then tied a rope to his ankles, looped it around a tree to where I was laying, and tied it off to my ankles. If he was trying to get loose, the rope would jerk on my ankles and wake me up. I told him that if I found him trying to escape, I would just kill him and be done with him. He told me that I needn't worry about that. He said he was a changed man now and had no desire for his old life. He said he'd met someone out on the desert that had brought a peace and change into his life. I asked him who it was, and he said he didn't know, as he never saw him. He said that he just heard his voice.

I asked the man why the one who spoke to him didn't take him to safety somewhere. He said that all the man said was that he would give him the strength to make it here if he changed his life from thieving and killing, so he promised he would change. I told him that if I ever saw him again after I got him to a settlement, I would take him even farther out into the desert and drop him off. He said that I would never have to worry about that, as he was going to head down south a couple of hundred miles to a ranch where the owner once told him that a job would always be open for him if he needed. He said that it would give him a chance to make a new start.

I said no more and walked away. All the things he said disturbed me. I'd had an experience similar back down the trail some time ago. I didn't understand it then, and didn't understand it now.

I waited another week, and then began the trek towards a settlement that I had heard was maybe a hundred miles south of where I was. The walk was hot and dry. We found another small water hole about half way there, so I refilled the water pouches, made coffee, and heated some biscuits and jerky. It was good. I set camp, as I decided the man still needed to get rest for him to be able to make it to the settlement.

After the second day at the water hole, we continued our way towards where the settlement was supposed to be. Three days later we arrived. I resupplied, and then made my way to the livery. Once there, I asked the liveryman if he knew of any horses for sale. He said that the only one he knew of was an old broken-down nag that a rancher had left with him. I asked to see it. We went around to the corral, and I found he had described the animal well.

Vanishing Anger

I asked him how much would he take for it. He just laughed, and then reached over and picked up a halter with rope from the fence. He handed it to me, and then said that I better get that damned nag off his property before he decided to make dog food out of it. He went on to say that all it was doing was eating his hay. I asked him if he had any old discarded saddles around, and he pointed towards a pile back behind the stable. I went over and picked out the best I could find, which wasn't much. There were several old blankets laying there, so I selected the best one of them as well. I asked how much, and again he laughed and said that I was saving him from having to haul them off. I spotted a lone bridle peeking out from under the pile. I pulled it out and found it was in pretty bad shape but usable. He gave that to me as well.

I then turned to the man that I brought with me, and told him to saddle up his horse so he could get on his way south. When he had the horse all rigged up, he mounted, and we headed to the mercantile. I bought him a bedroll, water pouch, and enough canned food to get him to his destination. I walked his mount over to the well, so he could fill his water pouch and let his horse satisfy its thirst. He also took his last drink before he departed towards his destination. Once he was all set to travel, I picked up the lead rope on my burro and the reins of the horse and led them to the south side of the settlement. I told him to ride and not turn back, because if I ever saw him again, I would kill him on the spot. I handed him the reins and he immediately headed south. I sat on the end of the boardwalk and watched until he was out of sight. I hoped that it would be the last time I ever saw him. I felt it would be, as the man sincerely sounded as though he was a changed man.

Chapter Twelve

I spent the next three days trying to buy another horse, but to no avail. In the end, I just made sure I had all the supplies I would need and headed back to camp. A week later, I arrived and found nothing out of place, so I settled in with the thought that this was going to be my life for a time. I made up a fire, and then took care of the burro. It now had become a habit to automatically put on a pot of coffee first thing. That damned stuff had almost become as good a buddy to me as the burro had. If that danged frontiersman ever showed his face again, I'd give him a chewing out about that. I chuckled with that thought.

I prepared all the items I would need for the next day to go and pan out all the gold I could before nightfall overtook me. I turned in early, as I was plum tuckered out from all that had gone on during the last couple of weeks. I might just as well have stayed up and drank the rest of that damned coffee, as sleep just wouldn't come. I tossed and turned till well after dark had settled over camp. When sleep did finally overcome me, it was a sound sleep. I didn't wake till well after the sun was up. I hadn't even heard my alarm clock. I quickly looked over to see if my burro was all right. It was. It had its head laying on the ground, with its eyes pasted on me with the look of "Just when the hell are you going to get your lazy butt up and get started?"

I just rolled over like I was going back to sleep. That burro got up and began braying the loudest I had ever heard it bray. It wouldn't quit until I got up and went over and whispered in its ear. What I whispered in its ear wasn't very nice and that damned burro must have understood me, as it backed away and turned its rear end towards me. With the look it had on its face, I hurriedly backed away, afraid it was going to kick me to kingdom come. It just stood there with a smirk on its face. Maybe he just wanted me to kiss his rear end. As far as I was concerned, it was one and the same. Either way, I wasn't going near that beast. I decided to stay in camp, as I didn't want to get near the burro until it had a change of heart and loved me again.

By noon, I could tell there had been a gradual change coming over the burro, so I grabbed a handful of grain and walked over to him. He still had that wild look in his eyes, but had decided to forgive me so it could have that grain. It seemed to do the trick. I began whispering in his ear that he was a good burro and we would go to the mine in the morning. He raised his head and nuzzled up and down on my cheek. All was well again.

I spent the rest of the day making repairs on my equipment where needed and, every once in a while, took out my scope and checked out the surrounding area around camp. I was always relieved when there was nothing but desert to see. I would sometimes scope the mountainside to see if I could spot any animals. I had seen deer a few times as they walked by my pool of gold.

When the next morning came, I made my meal and pot of coffee. After satisfying my belly, I packed the equipment up and placed it on the burro. We headed for a day of gathering gold. When we arrived, I picketed the burro and went right to work panning the gold out. I picked out all the nuggets that were visible, and poured the fines in a bag for taking back to camp to refine the flakes and powder gold from the ore during the evening. I generally got another ounce from that. I would do that for a week or so, then I would take a few days off to rest up.

After a couple of months had passed, I decided to make a trip to Beatty. I needed supplies, and the break would do me some good. I prepared everything for the trip and hid all my gold. I didn't want to use any of the gold to buy anything, as it would only tend to cause others to try to find where I was getting it. I still had a quantity of gold coins from the sale of the horses, saddles, and bottle of whisky.

I left early the next morning. I had become used to the walk, as it allowed me to see so much more of my surroundings, and it was peaceful. I came to enjoy all my surroundings. With a horse, I seemed to always be in a hurry. There was no hurrying a burro. They not only had a pace of their own, but a mind of their own as well.

On the first night, we camped at my spot where the old prospector was buried. After setting up camp, I took the lead rope off the burro and led it over to where the old prospector's grave was. It stood there with a forlorn look and brayed only twice. It then turned and wanted to return to the spring where I had been picketing it. I figured the pain from the loss of its old partner must be fading.

The next night I camped just outside of Beatty. When morning came, I led the burro over to the blacksmith's shop and had him check it over. He found the shoes worn, and one was worked loose. He replaced them. I then went to the eatery and had breakfast. When I was done with my meal, I left and went to the mercantile to supply up. As I entered, I got the surprise of my life. There, standing as big as a mountain, was the frontiersman I had left behind on my way here from the East Coast.

I walked up to him, extended my hand, and said, "Howdy, Long Knife!" He just stood there and stared at me. It dawned on me that I had grown a full beard since I left him and he didn't recognize me. I just stood there for a moment with a big grin on my face.

Finally, he blurted out, "Who the hell are you?"

I started laughing and said that my name was Randle. He still just stood there with a blank look on his face. I then opened my shirt and said, "Look! I got hair on my chest!"

All of a sudden, he burst out laughing so loud that everybody in the store was looking at us. Even some of those who had been outside within earshot came in to see what was so funny. He then grabbed my hand and about shook my arm out of its socket. When things settled down, we had to explain to everyone what it was all about. They all went off laughing as well.

We walked outside and sat down on a bench that was in front of the mercantile. I asked him how he'd been faring, and he said it had been a pretty rough go since we'd parted ways. He said he had fought Indians until he was sick of it. He remembered me and the fact that I was going to head northwest, so he had set out to find me. He said that he had crossed the river in the same place I had crossed, and found the body of a prospector with a bullet hole in his head. He said he had wondered if I had anything to do with it. I told him I did. I then explained what had happened. When I was done, he told me to remind him not to borrow any of my horses without telling me first. We laughed. He went on to say that he had tried to follow my tracks, but that they were few. He said that it took him several months to finally make his way to Beatty.

After a lull in the conversation, he reached over, tugged on my beard, and said that it was no wonder he didn't recognize me, as I didn't have that when he met me. We both laughed. I told him he didn't smell any different than he did after the rattler incident. We both laughed hard after that. When we calmed down, he said he had washed off really good when he crossed that river where I had left that prospector. He said that when he smelled that decaying body, he thought it was himself, so he'd scrubbed extra good with soap. He said that he was so clean that it made him sick, as he wasn't used to that. We laughed again.

He told me that he was in the process of asking questions about me when I had walked in. He had already asked the blacksmith and told him that he had found a dead prospector by a river. He said that he told the blacksmith that he had wondered if I had anything to do with it. He went on to say that the blacksmith had said I was indeed responsible for killing that skunk. The blacksmith was the one who sent him to the mercantile for information. What were the odds of us meeting like this? I told him that all I was going to do was supply up and leave. He asked me where I was going from here. I told him that I would be heading back towards a settlement on the other side of the mountain on the other side of the desert.

I asked him where he was off to. He asked me if I knew anything about what lay north of that settlement. I told him that the only thing I had heard about it was that there was a magnificent lake not too far north from there that they called Tahoe, and that I figured it was probably named that by the Indians. Long Knife sat silent for a moment, and then said that he felt he would like to go see that lake.

We again sat there in silence for a moment. He then asked me if I would mind if he tagged along with me to the other side of the mountain, and then he continued on to that settlement after parting company with me. I told him that I wouldn't mind at all, but only on one condition. He asked me what the condition was, and I told him there would be no more snake dancing. We both burst out with laughter. He told me that he couldn't promise me that, but he would do his best to dissuade the snakes from wanting to sleep with him. We both went into another belly-shaker.

He asked me when I was leaving, and I told him that I had intended to supply up, have a meal at the eatery, and then leave for the trail when I was done. I told him that I always camped at the bottom of this side of the mountain, and then headed over in the morning. He told me that he would do likewise. We went back in, purchased our supplies, and placed them in our respective packs. I had much more than he did, but I had told him that he would be able to resupply again at Lone Pine.

We left there and went to the eatery. When we finished eating, we left immediately for that trail. When we arrived, we wasted no time setting up camp. We elected to settle for pan biscuits and jerky. We drank a pot of that hair grower, and then turned in.

Morning came early, as my alarm clock went gone off. I looked over towards Long Knife, and there he sat wide-eyed and holding his firearm cocked and ready to shoot up the place. I began laughing so hard that I fell back down on my bedroll. When I had regained my composure, I had to explain to him about my alarm clock. We both began laughing. He asked me if there was any way I could not set my alarm, and again we both laughed. I told him that I had been trying to figure that out.

We built a fire and made pancakes and sausage. The coffee was on the fire, boiling away. When breakfast was consumed and the coffee pot was empty, we cleaned up, packed, and when Long Knife had his horse saddled, we left, heading up the trail towards the desert.

Chapter Thirteen

Once we had arrived back where the old prospector was buried, we made camp for the night. I got a fire going and placed a pot of coffee on. Long Knife made a meal of steak, potatoes, and corn. He decided to stay in camp with me until morning, when he would then depart for Lone Pine. I told him that the earlier he left the cooler it would be crossing the desert. He asked me if there was a way I could set the alarm an hour earlier. We laughed. We finished our meal, and then sat by the fire until the coffee was gone. It was still a little early, but we decided to turn in anyway.

It was pretty early when we woke up. I checked the animals while Long Knife got the fire going. Breakfast was steak and eggs. Once we had all the cook gear cleaned and packed, Long knife saddled his horse and mounted up. He stuck out his hand and we shook for what seemed a long time. I told him that if he ever made it back this way to leave word in Beatty where he would be and I'd try to look him up. He said that he doubted he would ever make it back down this way, as he had heard that there was a lot of territory that was unexplored

Vanishing Anger

up in the far north that he wanted to see. He wished me well and I wished him the same. I hated seeing him ride off, and was jealous of him at the same time. If it hadn't been my misfortune to inherit that cursed gold, I perhaps would be riding along with him.

I placed the packs back on the burro, and then headed for the mine camp. Once I was in camp and had everything put in its place, I checked my gold and found it was all there. I settled for just staying around camp for a couple of days to get well rested and relaxed. The gold wasn't going anywhere. Each day went by uneventfully. On the third day, I rose early and began a month-long push to get as much gold out of that pool as I could. It just seemed to replenish itself on a daily basis. By the end of the month, I had two heavy bags of nuggets and a bag and a half of flakes and dust.

I was getting low on some supplies, so I knew it was time to head to a settlement. I decided that I would go to that settlement that I had left the man who headed for that ranch south of the settlement. I placed all the gold in a pack sack, slid it back under the brush, and then covered it with sand. I kept the half bag of flakes and dust, and placed it in the pack on the burro. When everything was in place, I led the burro out of camp and began the trek towards the settlement. I had an ulterior motive for going to that particular settlement. The others were much closer.

A week later, I arrived and resupplied immediately. I went to the livery and had the shoes checked on the burro. They were found to be in good shape. I then asked the owner if he knew of a good horse for sale, and he said that they were pretty hard to come by in these parts. I asked him to hold one for me until I returned if one ever became available. He said he would.

I asked the blacksmith if he knew anything about that ranch about a hundred miles south of the settlement. He knew about it, and told me that the owner was as fine a man as he had ever become acquainted with. He told me that the rancher had been there just several days ago. He said the man looked pretty poorly. He had told him that he had left the ranch in the hands of the best hired hand he had ever had. That perked me up a little. I wondered. I thanked the blacksmith and headed to the eatery.

When my meal was complete, I headed south. I found a nice place to camp that was well secluded yet gave me good visibility of my surroundings. The blacksmith had told me that there was a band of Indians roaming around this way and that I should keep a wary eye for them. He said they were a pretty mean bunch. I hadn't seen any tracks so far, so I felt comfortable with the camp that I had chosen. I made a mental note not to let my guard down. I liked my hair too well to let it be had by them. I also had heard that they had a special liking for burro meat, and that was the last thing they would ever get from me. I had become pretty good friends with my burro.

I made a small smokeless fire, prepared my meal, and then put the fire out. No sense inviting those Indians to dinner. I turned in early, as I wanted an early start.

It was still dark when I woke up. For some reason, I had an uneasy feeling. I decided not to start a fire and settle for pan biscuits and jerky. I would do without coffee this morning. That proved to be harder than I thought it would be. I wanted my damned coffee. I tucked my spare .44 in my belt.

I made it to mid-morning before I decided to stop, make a pot of coffee, and heat the biscuits and jerky. Heating them always made them much tastier. As soon as the coffee was done, I extinguished the fire. I ate the hot jerky and biscuits, and then washed them down with the delectable coffee. I packed away the pot and began my trek south. After several miles had slipped by, I spotted the band of Indians in my path off at a distance.

They had spotted me as well and were following me off to the side. I dropped down into a draw, and then turned directly towards them. I felt they would think that I would make a run for it and not expect to see me right in front of them when I showed up. I tied the burro off to a scrub tree, the made my way towards the top of the draw. When I broke over the edge, I found myself standing in the middle of seven of them. I had both my .44s in my hands and wasted no time cutting them down. They were pretty well in disarray when I had popped up between them, so it made it pretty easy to wipe them out. I went around and made sure they were all dead.

Two of their ponies were standing nearby, so I made an attempt to capture one. The first one spooked, so I made another attempt for the other. It just stood there I easily took hold of its reins. I patted it on the shoulder and talked softly to it as I prepared to mount it. I had no problem. I decided to see if I could catch the others as well, and surprisingly captured the other six. I had rope on the pack that was on the burro, so I retrieved it and made halters for each of the ponies. I tied a lead rope on each one, and then led them over to the burro. I tied the lead ropes onto the burro's pack frame, and then mounted up and led the burro forward. The ponies fell right in line.

There were no problems with the ponies getting along with my burro, and I was happy about that. It took me another four days to make it to that ranch. I had no more trouble with the Indians. I had seen tracks, but never saw them, which made me glad.

As I rode up to the ranch house, a man stepped out onto his deck holding a shotgun. I stopped and yelled out that I was friendly and that I had just come to visit an old friend of mine. He asked me who that might be, and I told him that it was a mangy old cuss that rode this way a few months ago on an old swayback nag and on a worn-out saddle. I told him that he had come to work for him.

He slowly lowered the shotgun and walked my way with a painful limp. When he got near me, he asked me where I had gotten all the ponies. After I told him, he said for me to climb down so he could shake my hand. He said that those Indians had been causing trouble for quite some time and that I had done the folks around there a big favor. I asked him if he was in need of horses. He said yes, and that several of his neighbors would be interested as well.

He asked me how much I wanted for them, and I said that a good saddle along with a saddle blanket and a good bridle would be a great start. He said his neighbor had several extra saddles and blankets. He said he had an extra bridle. He then asked me what else I wanted. I said a couple of good warm blankets, and he told me he could come up with those. He then told me to get to the bottom line. He wanted to know how much I wanted for each one. I said that if and when he came up with all that I asked of him, the ponies were his. He asked me what the catch was, and I said that there was no catch, that was all I wanted.

I walked over to him and we shook hands. He told me to strip my animals and turn them loose in the corral. I watered them, and then did as he said. While I was heading with the man to his ranch house, I spotted a rider off in the distance heading towards us. The man said that he was the one I had come to see. He said for us to go on into the house and we could surprise the man when he saw me. We went inside, and the man poured me a cup of coffee, which tasted mighty good. He told me to slide over in and behind the door.

His hired hand walked up on the porch and made his way into the house. He stopped in front of the owner and was about to say something, when the owner told him to turn around and say howdy to an old friend. When he turned around and spotted me, he turned white as a ghost and started shaking. I held out my hand and told him howdy. He slowly extended his hand. I took hold of it, and, while shaking it, told him it was good to see him again. He asked me if I was there to kill him. I laughed and said that I was only here to see how he was getting along and if he needed anything. He said I didn't owe him anything. He went on to say that he had been a pretty bad hombre back in the desert but was truly a changed man now. He turned towards the owner for support. The owner said that he was the best and most trustworthy cowhand he had ever hired. The owner told him to join us for a cup of coffee.

After things had become a little less tense, the owner told him that he needed him to ride over to the neighbor and pick up a couple of items for him. He asked the owner what he needed those items for, as he didn't have anything to put it on. The owner told him to come with us. We rose and headed for the door. He walked over to the corral, and the hired hand was shocked at what he saw. The owner explained everything to him, and then told him to go on and get those items. The hired hand went to his horse and mounted up. He wasted no time heading out.

A little over an hour later, he returned with the other rancher, riding in a wagon with the items I wanted. He went right up to the corral and let out a whistle. He just kept saying "I'll be damned!" over and over again. He finally turned to me and we shook hands. He wanted to hear the whole story, so after retiring to the house I filled him in on all the details over coffee.

Chapter Fourteen

It was time for me to make my way back to my pool of gold. I hadn't mentioned a word about my find, but I did drag out the half bag of flakes and dust. When I showed that to them, their eyes widened. The owner asked me why I felt a need to show them. I told him that I had a motive. I went on to say that, if he had spare beef to butcher, I would sure like to buy a half. He said he could spare a half and would keep the other half for himself. I then asked him how his hired hand was doing financially. He said that with what little he could pay him, above a place to stay and his meals, that all he could do was scratch out enough money to occasionally buy a new shirt or maybe a new pair of boots. Money had been tight. He went on to say that he wasn't able to herd any of his cattle to market because of that marauding band of Indians. He told me that had all changed by my visit.

I handed the pouch of gold to the rancher and said that with that he just might be able to be a little more generous. He went on to ask what I wanted in return for it. I told him that I had no need for it and that I truly appreciated what he was doing for his hired hand. I don't know why I felt the way I did about his hired hand, except that I had gone through a similar experience and could relate to the change that overcame him.

The rancher then said that he had another spread just beyond this one that was pretty close to being as good as this one was. He told me that if I ever became interested in ranching that he would give it to me. He said that it was all he could do to keep up with one. He went on to say that because he had no children or any living relatives, he was turning this ranch over to the hired hand when he decided he couldn't handle it anymore. I told him that I might just take him up on that offer some day.

I rose to leave, and the rancher followed me out the door and over to the corral. His hired hand was leaning on the corral fence admiring the ponies. The rancher told him that after I had my chosen pony sorted out that he should pick one out for himself to replace the broken down old nag that he had been riding. We all laughed. I walked over and picked out a saddle, along with a bridle and blanket. The saddle that I had chosen had a nice set of saddlebags tied on the backend of it. I tossed the saddle over the fence rail, handed the bridle to the hired hand, and asked

Vanishing Anger

him to slip it on the pretty black-and-white pony. He said that he would have chosen that one if I hadn't. It was a beautiful horse, and probably only about three or four years old. It was also the largest pony in the herd. I told him that was the penalty for his sinful past. We once again all burst out with laughter.

The hired hand placed the bridle on the pony and led it over to the fence. He grabbed the saddle blanket, placed it on the back of the pony, reached over and picked up the saddle, and then strapped it on. He then led it to the rail gate and opened it. Once clear of the gate, he led the pony over to me and handed me the reins. I then asked him to retrieve my burro and pack frame. He handed the lead rope to me and said for me to slow down, as I was working him harder than he did for the rancher. The rancher said that he had been noticing that. We all burst out with laughter once again.

I mounted up and tied the lead rope off to the saddle horn. I reached up, took hold of the reins, and then extended my hand to the rancher. I told him that if he ever got up my way that he should look me up. I told him that his hired hand knew where I was located. I then reached over and shook hands with the hired hand. I told him to ride up and say howdy some time. He asked me if I was going to shoot him, and I told him that those days were in the past. I said for him to let bygones be bygones.

I turned my horse towards the settlement, with the intention of supplying up for an extended stay at the pool of gold. With the beef that I now had, I would not need any venison for a time. It was a great feeling riding a horse again. When I reached the settlement, I wasted no time in locating the blacksmith. I had him check the shoes and hoofs of the burro, and then had him trim the hooves and put shoes on my new horse. He had to hobble the horse, as it went a little wild when he began trying to trim the hooves. It had never had to endure the process before. It took a little extra time, but the blacksmith finally accomplished the task. I paid him extra for his troubles. He said that the Indians would just use their tomahawks to chop off the excess part of the hooves.

I thanked him, and then left for the mercantile. Once supplied up, I headed for the eatery. When I was done eating, I wasted no time getting on the trail towards my camp.

When I reached the spring that was approximately halfway to my camp, I noticed that someone else had discovered the spring

Vanishing Anger

and had stayed for at the least one night. That made me feel uneasy.

I spent the night and was on the trail again early in the morning. Something didn't feel quite right. I grew tenser as I rode nearer to my camp. When my camp finally came into sight, I became extremely cautious. I circled wide around the entire camp. I saw nothing out of place, so I began a slow approach towards the entrance. I rode off at a distance to where the small back entrance was. I dismounted and slowly approached the patch of greenery. I had my .44 in my hand, cocked and ready for whatever I encountered.

Once I was close enough, I tied the horse off to the small tree, and then slowly and silently entered the small opening. As I neared the interior, I reached out and slowly parted the branches to be able to get a good look around. It disgusted me when I saw that someone had indeed been here, but even worse, had wiped me out of everything and destroyed whatever was left. That angered me to no end. I went over immediately to the location where my gold was stashed and dug it up. It was intact. That was a relief, though it didn't cause my anger to subside one bit. Whoever it was had taken all my mining equipment, including the lantern. I cherished that lantern. The jar of lamp oil was gone as well.

I walked back out of the small opening and worked my way around to the main entrance. As I glanced the area over, I could see that whoever it was had left here only a short time ago. There was still some moisture left in the tracks in the sand that were in the shade just inside of the entrance. I took out my scope and scanned the area in the direction the tracks were headed. I saw nothing, but I knew that whoever it was wasn't far away.

I led the animals back inside of the camp and immediately began offloading the supplies. I was now intent on getting vengeance on whoever it was. As soon as everything was in its place, I picketed the burro, mounted up, and then headed out of the opening. It appeared that the rider was headed in the direction of my camp to the north on the mountain where I had buried the old prospector. I rode towards the mountains in a northeasterly direction, so as not to be easily detected.

I was pushing my horse a little harder than I should have, but I needed to get in front of that skunk. When I reached the mountain's edge, I worked myself uphill so I could keep some greenery between the thief and me. As I rode over each ridge, I took out my scope and scanned the desert floor. When I was within a mile or so of the camp, I topped another ridge. When I stopped, I took out the scope to have a look around. As I went to put the scope up, I was shocked to see the rider not more than a hundred feet from me. He was sitting there staring at me. His packhorse was overloaded. I waved as if there was nothing wrong. He waved back.

He must have thought it was a friendly encounter, as he rode straight towards me. When he drew near me, I spotted the lantern hanging on the side of the pack on the packhorse. I did everything I could to hide my anger. He sensed something was wrong and went for his sidearm. I drew with the speed of lightning and nailed him in the throat. He missed his gun with his hand and automatically grabbed for his neck. He sat there with a startled look on his face. His hands slipped down away from his neck, and the blood gushed out through the opening. He slowly began slipping over to one side and fell out of the saddle, landing on his head. He was dead.

I dismounted and walked over to his horse. After removing the thief's gun belt, I went through his pockets and took everything of value. I then picked up the reins and led his animals over to my horse. I mounted up and led them back towards my camp. I didn't bother to bury the scumbag. He didn't deserve it.

As I rode past him, I said two words over his still body: "Good riddance!" I rode on, and my anger subsided immediately. I was surprised about that, as in the past it would have a tendency to linger for a month or more.

I arrived in camp just as it was turning dark. I offloaded the animals and picketed them near the spring. I gave each one a good rubdown and gave them each a small bait of grain. They didn't look to be any worse for wear. I let all the gear lie where it was. I would wait to sort it all out in the morning. I was plum tired and didn't even bother to build a fire or eat. I turned in immediately.

When morning came, I was surprised, as I had not heard my alarm clock go off, and it was already full sunup. I glanced around; everything seemed to be in order. A hunger pang hit me, so a fire was the first order of business, followed by coffee, and close behind would be breakfast.

When all that was completed, I began the task of sorting out all the gear. All of the items that were not destroyed were intact, so I put them all away in their proper places. My supplies were now nearly doubled. The thief

Vanishing Anger

had some eggs and bacon, so I placed them near the spring along with mine to keep them cool. I looked over at the lantern, and it brought a smile to my face. I liked that lantern nearly as much as I liked my coffee. I took the rest of the day off. I would get back to the pool in the morning.

Chapter Fifteen

My scope had become my constant companion. The first thing every morning, I walked the perimeter of my camp and scoped out the surrounding area. If everything didn't look in order, I would immediately seek out what it was. Better safe than sorry. I started my fire and put a pot of coffee on. I then made and consumed a good breakfast of steak and eggs. I spent the day going over everything and repairing everything that needed it. I felt good to just relax without any outside disturbances. If it wasn't for the boredom that would inevitably set in, I would do the same for the next week or more. I decided that I would head for the pool in the morning.

When my alarm went off in the morning, I wasted no time getting finished with breakfast and loading up the burro. I took up his lead rope and headed for the pool. Once I arrived, I found everything in order, so I went into the cave and began picking out all the nuggets that I could see. After a couple of hours, I filled several of the bags with ore and headed back to camp. Once there, I went right into panning out the ore. By the time I had it all panned out, the day was over. Between the nuggets, flakes, and powder, I guessed I had gathered another three or four ounces of gold. It was so easy that I was becoming unimpressed with the value of the gold.

It had become a ritual to go to the pool, and then return and pan out the gold. I always buried the majority of the nuggets, placed a certain amount in small leather pouches, and then placed them in my spare pack sacks. I would place the packsacks under the brush over by the spring. I always tried concealing them the best I could. It didn't seem there would ever be an end to all the gold that was in the pool.

After several more weeks of getting out the gold, I decided I needed to shed the extra horses, as they had become a nuisance. I prepared camp for my departure in the morning. Once I had everything in order, I turned in for the night.

When my alarm went off, I immediately set my wheels in motion. I started the fire, and then made and consumed my breakfast, along with downing a pot of coffee. I saddled my pony and placed all the other gear on the horses I had. When satisfied that everything was in place, I headed for Beatty.

It was a struggle keeping peace between the horses and the burro. Once I reached the trail, I set camp for the night. While I was cooking my meal, a man walked up to me and asked if I minded if he rested for a spell. I offered him coffee and a meal. He accepted. I asked him why he was on foot. He told me that his horse had stumbled and broken a leg, so he had to put it down. I then asked him what he did with all of his gear. He said he hid it off to the side of the trail down towards Lone Pine just before you enter the desert.

He spotted all the horses I had with me and offered to buy one. He said he would give me three hundred for one, and it didn't take me but a second to tell him that I would let him have the packhorse for that money. He was plum pleased with that, and so was I. I then asked him if he might be interested in the other one. He said he might be. He got up, walked over to the horses, and looked them over. He turned to me and asked me how much I would take for the pony. I told him that it wasn't for sale until the other horse was sold. He asked me how much for both of them along with the saddles. I told him to make me an offer. He pulled out a pouch of gold coins and spread them out in front of me. He had twelve hundred dollars laying there. He asked me if that was enough for all the horses along with their gear. I told him the burro didn't go with them. He said that would be fine. I asked him if he was sure he wanted to do that, and he answered by asking me again if that was enough. I told him that it was a deal, and then gathered up the gold coins and placed them inside of my shirt.

The man went over to the pony and placed the saddle on it. He then placed the packboard on the packhorse and the saddle on the last horse. He mounted the pony, rode over to me, and then stopped. He held out his hand and I shook it. I asked him what he was going to do with all the horses. He put on a big grin and said he would double his money up north of Beatty a far piece. He left, heading down the trail towards where he had his saddle stashed away. An hour later, he came riding back by with his saddle strapped on the packhorse. That pretty much confirmed all he had told me. I waved as he rode on by. He waved with a big grin on his face. I reached down and placed the safety strap back on my .44. I had found out the hard way about trusting strangers in these parts.

I decided to pack up and head back towards camp. I made it to the camp where the old prospector was buried as it turned dark. After taking care of the burro, I turned in. It was a total relief to be back to just my good friend and me. I would never in my life have felt comfortable with walking before I began this incredible journey looking for peace and tranquility. I believed I had truly achieved my goal. I was at peace and extremely content with all that surrounded me and everything I had found to fill my days. I had proven that I could survive most everything that danger could throw at me.

I fell into a deep, sound sleep. When I awoke, the sun was well up and the heat of the day was already climbing towards its peak.

I wasn't in a hurry to head to the pool of gold. It would still be there when I decided that I wanted to begin gathering the gold from its bowels. I rose up and checked my failing alarm clock, finding him to be doing well. I went back and started a fire, and then set about placing the coffee on to boil. I don't know why it has to take so long to be ready. By the time my meal had been prepared and consumed, the coffee was in a full boil. I took the egg shells and tossed them into the pot to settle the coffee grounds. The frontiersman had taught me that little trick. That thought perked me up a little. I wondered where he'd ended up. I decided to make the trek over to Lone Pine and ask around about him.

I packed up and headed in that direction. It was dark when I arrived. I made camp just outside of the settlement. I'd go in when morning came around. I made a small fire and cooked up a steak. That and the coffee that I still had left over from this morning would be enough to tide me over until morning. I would have breakfast at the eatery when morning came. I cleaned everything up and packed it away so I would be ready to head on into the settlement after I woke up. I laid out my bedroll, and then turned in for the night. Sleep came quickly and was very peaceful.

When my alarm went off, I was up and ready for whatever the day would bring. I packed up and headed straight for the eatery. Breakfast was good. I asked the lady about the frontiersman, and she excitedly told me that he might still be in or around the settlement. He had been in the night before for dinner. I told her that if she saw him to tell him that his old friend with hair all over his chest was looking for him. She got a serious look on her face, so I had to explain what that was all about. She then began laughing. It continued all the way to the kitchen. She came back out with another pot of coffee and refilled everyone's cup. She was chuckling continually until she arrived at my table. She began laughing hard again and had to sit down. Once she settled down enough, she reached over and refilled my cup. She then told me that she wasn't too kind about what she had been thinking before I had explained it all to her. She apologized for having such a dirty mind. That got me to laughing, and in turn, she began again.

I finished my coffee and headed for the mercantile. Once there I again asked about a frontiersman by the name of Long Knife. It was the same story from them. He mentioned that Long Knife had said he was camped just north of the settlement. I thanked the man and headed out the door.

I went over to the livery and asked the blacksmith about Long Knife. He basically told me the same thing. I then headed north out of the settlement looking for the Long Knife. I did a crisscross search, so I wouldn't be so likely to miss him if he was still in the area. I located a fresh camp that had been used overnight. The fire pit ashes were still hot. I searched for signs all around the camp and located a set of tracks that were headed in a northerly direction. I knew I would never catch up to him, with me towing a burro and him riding a

Vanishing Anger

horse. I headed back to the livery and inquired about buying a horse. He said he had an old swayback one that was still healthy enough to ride. I asked him how much he wanted for the old nag, and he said it would cost me three hundred dollars. That shocked me.

I asked him what it would cost for me to rent the horse from him. He grinned and said that it would be cheaper for me to buy the animal. I then asked him if the animal came with a blanket, saddle, and a set of reins. He told me that I could have whatever I found out back in the discarded pile. I reluctantly shelled out the gold. There wasn't a decent saddle in the entire pile. I picked through them and, in the end, came up with all that I needed. I carried them inside and placed everything on the horse. I was outfitted with a worse horse than the one I had stuck the man with that I took out of the desert. It was humiliating!

Chapter Sixteen

I left the settlement, leading my burro with my coat pulled up and wrapped around my face so no one would see my embarrassment. I began my search for Long knife. I relocated Long Knife's tracks and followed them. I rode faster than I should have, but I wanted to make up as much ground as I could between Long Knife and me. I could tell the tracks were becoming fresher and fresher.

I crossed a small stream and saw that water was still seeping into the tracks. I knew I was close. After another mile or so, I finally spotted him up on a hillside about three or four hundred yards away. I let out a war whoop that could be heard for quite a distance. Long Knife grabbed his .44 and wheeled around facing me. I kept riding towards him, and when I was within a distance where he finally recognized me, he began laughing so hard that I thought he would fall out of the saddle.

I rode on up to his side and extended my hand. We shook hands. He began laughing again. I asked him what was so funny. He then said that he saw that horse at the livery, and the owner that brought it in asked the blacksmith if he would butcher the animal for dog food, and the blacksmith told the man that he didn't want all the dogs in the area vomiting all over the place. The owner had turned and left, telling the blacksmith to do whatever he wanted to with the animal. He then asked me how I came about getting stuck with the nag. I told him that I had bought it for three hundred dollars. Long Knife began howling with laughter. When he settled down, he said that there was a sucker born every minute. I told him that it wasn't funny. He howled with laughter again.

When Long Knife settled back down, he apologized and said that I would probably have reacted in the same manner if he had bought the animal. I told him that he was probably right. We both chuckled for a short time. He then asked me what brought me up this way. I told him that the only reason that I came looking for him was to ask him a question. I opened my shirt and exposed my chest. With my best poker face look on, I asked him if all the hair on my chest would go away if I quit drinking coffee.

He sat there staring at me for what seemed like an hour with a dumbfounded look on his face. He then blurted out, "Are you serious?"

With the same poker face look on my face, I just said, "Yup!"

He stuttered around for a minute, and then said with an uncertain voice, "Hell, I don't know!" He didn't know what to say or how to react.

I just sat there with that poker face look and said nothing. I finally couldn't hold it back any more. That look on Long Knife's face got to me. I burst out with laughter so hard that it was all I could do to stay in the saddle.

He sat there looking at me for a long time, and then finally said, "You're crazy! You're just plain loco!" He started laughing with me, and our laughter got so bad that we both had to get down off our horses to keep from falling.

Once we settled down and were sitting on the ground, he said that I had really gotten him good on that one. I asked him if we were even now, and he said we were and stuck out his hand. I took hold of his hand and we shook for a long time. I then asked him if he had any more questions. He held his hands in the air and said no, there was no way he would be able to top that one. We began laughing again.

He said we might just as well find a place to set camp, as we weren't going to get anywhere today. We found a nice little spot nestled in among some small pines with a small stream flowing through it. After offloading and taking care of the animals, we set up a canvas shelter and stowed our bedrolls and gear under it. We built a fire ring, made up a nice fire, and gathered enough wood to last for several days. Daylight was starting to fade, so we made our meal. When we were done, we started sipping coffee while sitting around our campfire. I told him that I wanted to take a break from prospecting and had thought about trying to find him to see what it was like meandering around looking for nothing to do.

He burst out in a loud voice, asking if that's all I thought he was doing. He went on to say it was hard work looking for nothing to do. We laughed. I went on to tell him that I had been pretty lucky finding gold here and there, but that I wanted to find something I could enjoy doing when I had all the gold I needed to make it till the end of my days. He told me to show him the gold and that, just maybe, he could help me to the end of my days. We laughed hard with that one.

He asked me how long I planned to be away from my prospecting. I told him as long as he could stand me. He asked me what time I was leaving in the morning and burst out laughing. I told him I didn't think that was funny, and with that poker-faced look, I started getting up like I was leaving. He got that serious look on his face again.

I burst out laughing, and then told him, "What's the matter? Can't a man go relieve his bladder without someone worrying about it?" I laughed again.

He yelled back, "You and your damned poker face is enough to worry anybody." We both laughed.

When I had finished relieving myself, I returned to the fire, poured myself another cup of coffee, and then sat back down across from Long Knife. He looked at me with a serious face and said, "I thought you said we were even."

All I said was "Oops!" We laughed hard again.

We sat up until late into the night, talking about everything we both had been doing and what our plans were for the future. When the coffee was gone, we stoked up the fire and turned in for the night. Sleep came quickly.

When morning came, my alarm went off. Long Knife came bounding out of his bedroll with his .44 in his hand, yelling, "What the hell was that?"

As I built up the fire again, I told him that it was my alarm. I then had to explain all about my burro. He told me that I should shoot my damned alarm. I checked on all the animals, and then went back by the fire. Long Knife had the coffee on and breakfast cooking. It would be pancakes and eggs. It hit the spot.

Once we were finished with breakfast and had everything cleaned and packed, we loaded up the animals and mounted up. We began winding our way up the mountainside. Long Knife told me he had located a beautiful location where the view was astounding. He planned on building a small cabin somewhere in that area. He went on to say that it was where we were heading.

Sometime in the mid-afternoon, we leveled out near the top of the ridge and came to the location he had told me about. It was indeed one of the most magnificent views I had ever seen. Off in the distance was a tall and awe-inspiring waterfall. The valley below had a stream meandering through it. I told him he had a dream home in his vision. I also said I was envious of him. We rode a little farther up the ridge to a place that was perfect for his cabin.

We dismounted and stood side by side admiring all that lay in front of us. I turned to him and asked when he planned on starting his cabin. He said that, until I had showed up, he was planning to begin immediately. I told him that he needn't let my presence stop him. I went on to say that if he didn't mind, I would like to stay and give him a hand until it was finished and he had moved in. He told me he would be plum tickled by that.

We began immediately gathering large stones that would be used for the foundation blocks. Once they were all in place, we went a distance over the ridge and found a grove of lodge pole pines. We spent two days felling the trees and trimming all the branches off. Once we had enough logs, we used the horses to drag them back over to the building site. We then cut them all to the desired lengths. That took another day.

The real excitement came when we began the next morning notching the logs out to fit on top of each other. As the walls were slowly rose and the cabin began taking shape, Long Knife stopped. We stood there looking at each other and he said, "It's going to be a fabulous place to live, and if I ever decide that I wanted to locate in this area, there would be room for a neighbor nearby." We stood there smiling at each other.

We went back to work. Once the walls were up and we had the long poles ready for the roofing, we began that task. We were now ready to find some cedar trees for making the shakes for the roof. To find them, we had to ride clear down to the bottom of the valley. We found two windfalls that looked like they had been down for several years. We cut the logs to lengths of approximately four feet. The logs were about three feet across.

I suggested to Long Knife that we should place our ropes around the end of a length and drag it up to the cabin whole, as it would save us a lot of trips packing the split shakes. He agreed. However, when we tried to pull a section up the hill, it was too much for one animal. We then put both our ropes around one section and dragged that to the top. That worked much better.

After we had dragged the last section up from the valley, we sat down to a good meal, proud of our accomplishment. We quit early and just sat discussing everything that we needed to do in the morning. I suggested that he begin trimming out all the windows and the door, while I split the shakes out of the logs. He agreed.

When morning came and the alarm went off, I checked the animals, and then returned to find Long Knife just finishing stoking up the fire. I cooked breakfast while Long Knife put the coffee together and placed the pot against the fire. Breakfast was good. The coffee was even better. I noticed Long Knife staring at me, so I opened my shirt and smiled at him. He laid back, laughing his fool head off. He said that if I kept drinking that coffee, someone would mistake me for a grizzly bear someday and shoot my big butt. We laughed long and hard. Long Knife and I were becoming pretty good friends. I was enjoying our time together. I felt I just might take him up on his offer of becoming his neighbor.

We spent the next two days finishing the construction. We then went down in the valley and looked along the stream until we found a clay seam. I devised a travois out of some small lodge pole pines and had it strapped onto Long Knife's horse. I would have been glad to use my horse, but it wasn't long for this world and I didn't want to up the departure time. We loaded all the clay onto the travois that we felt the horse could pull up the long, steep hillside. After two trips, we began the task of building the hearth and caulking the seams between the logs of the walls of the cabin.

When dusk began to close in on us, we quit for the day. We completed our meal and turned in early, as we were absolutely tuckered out from all that we had done that day.

When the dawn arrived and breakfast was put behind us, we finished the task of caulking. We had to make one more trip down to the river because we ran out of clay. The cabin was now complete, and it was a beauty.

Chapter Seventeen

When the following morning rolled around and we had completed breakfast, I told Long Knife that I felt the need to get back to prospecting. He asked me how long it would be before I felt I had enough to settle down into a life such as his. I told him that greed had a grip on me right now and I had been finding quite a bit of gold. I told him I was waiting for that point where the greed and need wore off. I said that I didn't feel I was far from it.

He looked long and hard at me, and then said, "I know from studying your face that you've struck it rich somewhere. I don't care about where your find is, but I hope you soon have more than enough so you can set it aside and come on up and join me in this paradise. You can always go back to it if you feel the need. It's not going to go anywhere."

I just sat there smiling at him. I told him he just might be right, but right now, I felt the need to get back. He asked me when I was pulling out. I stood up and said that right now was as good a time as any. He helped me place all the gear on my animals. When we were done, I mounted up and reached out to shake hands with him. He told me to be safe and come back soon and often. I said I would, and then wheeled around and left.

I stopped off in Lone Pine and stocked up on supplies. I then wasted no time heading out across the desert to my pool of gold. It would be fun to get back. I now didn't have a care in the world, and I was in no hurry to be anywhere. I arrived in camp in the dark of night. I had a bright moon for light, and when I entered camp, I immediately lit the lantern. I looked around and found nothing out of place, so I offloaded the animals and picketed them over by the spring. I was tired, so I turned in immediately.

It turned out to be a sound sleep, as the sun was full up when I awoke. I spent the day putting everything in its place and gathering all my trash to bury a distance from camp. I took out my scope and made my usual rounds outside of camp looking for anything out of place. I sat down facing the mountain range and scoped it out. I saw several herds of deer and spotted one bear.

When I returned to the fire, I looked over towards the pool, and when I saw my horse, I decided that I was going to saddle him up and place the packboards on the burro, as I felt a need for some fresh venison.

I began the climb, following an animal trail that was north of where the pool of gold was. I worked my way towards where I had spotted the largest herd of deer. I had counted six or seven deer at the time. I knew they would bed down on an outcropping that overlooked the draw below them. I had to circle wide so I wouldn't be spotted and spook them out of the area. As luck would have it, I spotted a large doe about fifty yards away, over on the hillside across the draw from me that I had been working my up through. That would save me a lot of time and work. I withdrew my rifle from the scabbard, and with the first shot had my meat down on the ground.

I rode over and dressed it out. I cut it into manageable pieces and loaded it onto the burro. It was a heavy doe. I would have plenty of fresh meat. I rolled the hide up, loaded it on the burro as well, and headed back to camp. I had a lot of jars that had been used for canned goods, so I cut the meat up and placed as much as would fit into each jar, and then placed them in the shallow end of the pool where the cold water of the spring came up from the ground. I would make jerky out of what I had left over. I kept two nice-sized roasts for cooking right away, and several steaks that I would use for breakfast over the next few days. It would all be mighty tasty.

It turned dark, so I ate a biscuit and a couple of pieces of jerky that I heated over the fire. After chasing it down with the leftover coffee, I turned in for the night.

When morning came, my alarm went off much earlier than I wanted it to, but I guessed I was destined to live out my days with it. I rose, stoked up the fire, and then began preparing my breakfast of venison steak and eggs. I placed a fresh pot of coffee on the fire. Once my meal was complete, I began the task of loading my needed items for recovering the gold from the pool. In all probability, I already had enough gold buried a couple of feet deep in behind the pool to enable me to live luxuriously in some city anywhere in the world for the rest of my days. I guess that's what greed does to a person. You always want more.

I took up the lead rope of the burro and headed to the pool. I spent the next three weeks taking out as much gold as I could. There seemed to be a never-ending supply washing down into the pool from the underground stream that fed it.

It was time for another break from the ritual that I had placed myself in. After much thought, I decided that I had yet to venture over the mountain range that lay west of Lone Pine, so that's what I decided that I would do for the next few months. I secured my camp, and then packed all my belongings on the burro. I tied my bedroll onto the back of my saddle. After I was sure that everything was ready, I placed the saddle on my horse and mounted up for my new adventure.

After reaching Lone Pine, I spent the night just outside of the settlement. When morning rolled around and my alarm had gone off, I packed up and headed for the eatery. When I was done with breakfast, I headed to the livery, where the owner came out to greet me. He had a hungry look on his face. He held the reins of my horse while I stepped down. We shook hands like we were long-lost friends. I don't know why, as all he had ever done was rip me off for all the money he could get. That's how I had ended up with the swayback old nag I was harnessed with. I asked him to check the shoes on both of my animals, as I would be heading on up over the mountain towards the west.

He looked at me long and hard with a sheepish grin on his face. He said that I should consider trading in my old dilapidated nag for a better horse. He said that he didn't think my horse could make it to the top, let alone over to the other side. He went on to say that he had a good, stout, young horse he could turn loose of, and he would give me a good trade-in for my horse. I asked him how much he wanted for his horse. He played with his beard for a moment like he was in deep thought, and then said he could let me have it cheap, as I was a prior customer. I asked him how much cheap was. Again, he swirled his beard around in his fingers, and then said he would let me have it for four hundred dollars. I didn't say a word. I just stood there staring at him.

After a moment or two, I told him that I thought he was a little steep with his price. He then told me again that he would give me a good trade-in for my horse. I asked him how much. He swirled his beard around as before, and then said he would give me a little extra for it. I asked him just how much extra he was talking about. He again twirled his beard around and said with a sheepish grin that he would give me top dollar. I again asked him how much top dollar was. With the same actions as before, he finally blurted out "fifty dollars." I almost choked on that, but kept the same poker face. I knew from the beginning that he was trying to rip me off once more. I told him that I would have to think it over for a little bit.

I then told him to go ahead and replace all the shoes on the animals, as I felt they needed it anyway. I told him that if I did buy the horse, that I would probably keep my old one for a backup when I returned. I asked him if I could board my old horse there until I did come back, and he said that he got a dollar a day for that. I said that it sounded fair. I asked him about when my animals would be ready, and he told me to come back in a couple of hours.

I left for the mercantile to supply up on the few items I needed to get over the top to the next settlement. I asked the owner all the questions I could think of about what lay ahead for me. He was extremely knowledgeable about it, and told me of a trail that lay just south a couple of miles and was a much safer way to cross over. I welcomed that piece of information. It was now time to go back to the stable. I picked up my supplies and headed for it.

When I arrived, the liveryman was just leading my horse out to the corral. I noticed it was limping pretty badly. I went over and asked him what was bothering my horse so bad. He just shrugged his shoulders and said that sometimes horses limped like that for a couple of days until they get used to the new shoes. I reached over and picked up the horse's

Vanishing Anger

leg and looked at its hoof. The whole hoof was split clear into the center tissue. I put its leg back down, and with a scowl, told him he had ruined my horse. He tried to tell me that it came in that way.

I drew my sidearm and said slowly but clearly that he had just bought himself a horse. He stated he would give me the fifty he offered. With a mean, scornful look, I said again that he was going to give me another horse in its place. He stuttered that he only had one other horse. I told him that it would do. He tried to argue with me, and my anger was beginning to well up. He could see that. I cocked the hammer back on my .44 and told him to write up a bill of sale immediately. He knew he was a dead man if he didn't. His little scam hadn't gone quite like he intended.

I made him write it up stating that the horse came with a new saddle and blanket, and that the shoes on the burro were free. I then told him to mark it as paid in full, and then sign it. He did, without further argument. I stuffed the bill of sale down deep in my pocket. Funny what a cocked, fully-loaded .44 will do to convince a man to do what he is told. He asked me what I was going to do with the old nag. I told him that I was donating it to him.

I placed the new saddle on my new mount. I removed the saddlebags and rope from my old saddle, along with the rifle and scabbard, and then placed them on my new one. I placed the packboards and all my supplies on the burro, and then rode out towards the south from the settlement, chuckling as I did.

Chapter Eighteen

When I reached the trail the mercantile owner had told me about that led the way over the mountain range, I turned up it and rode directly towards the mountainside. When the trail began its ascent towards the crest, I continued until dusk came over the trail. Not knowing what lay ahead, I decided to make camp for the night.

It was a good night's sleep that I put behind me, and being that I had not eaten anything since I left Lone Pine the day before, I made a breakfast consisting of pancakes and sausage with syrup. It was satisfying. As usual, the coffee was good.

When I was finished, I continued my way up the winding trail. It was a long way to the crest, but finally reached it in the late afternoon. The animals and I were glad. It had been a long and grueling climb. I began my descent slowly, as it is always harder on the animals going downhill.

After spending another night about three-fourths of the way down, I finally reached the flat plains again. While I was up on the mountainside, I saw several settlements scattered towards the west and north. The largest ones were towards the northwest. That's the direction I chose to go. I had a purpose for wanting a larger settlement.

When I reached the largest one that I had seen from the mountain, I looked for and found a livery. It didn't take long to find one, as there were several. This was a center for prospectors and any other travelers that came along. The liveryman told me that they had discovered a lot of gold in the area. He said that that was the reason the settlement had grown so large. I walked away chuckling. *If they only knew.*

I went to the bank with the intention of selling off the gold I had, which was a considerable amount. The liveryman had told me to watch out for their scamming tendencies. It didn't take long to find out what he was talking about. I guess there was so much gold coming into the bank that they felt they only had to offer about seventy percent of what it was worth. I left without doing business with them.

I found a hotel, and spent the night taking advantage of a bath and soft bed that they had to offer. There was an eatery across the street. While eating there, I thought about what the liveryman had told me. He said that if I had

Vanishing Anger

the time I would do much better up north and west towards an ocean. He said that there was a large city there that provided all that one would need.

When breakfast was consumed, I went back to the hotel and checked out. I then went back to the livery and settled with the owner. I loaded all my gear and left for that city he had told me about. Not knowing where I was going, it took me three days to reach it. It didn't take me long to figure out why I had left the shipping docks back east. I wanted out of the area as fast as I could settle my affairs.

After boarding my horse and burro, I found a hotel and stowed my gear away. I left immediately in search of a reputable bank. The hotel clerk had put me on to one, so I wasted no time in finding it. I sold them my gold at a fair rate, and then asked for a bank draft for the entire amount. They only charged me a fair fee for the service. I asked them if they had an envelope to put the bank draft in, and the clerk handed one to me. I offered to pay, and the clerk told me that he should have put the draft in one to begin with. I thanked him and left for my hotel room.

I borrowed a pen from the clerk and a piece of paper to write a note on. I dipped the quill into the container of ink, and then scribbled a note to the folks that I had given my home to back on the East Coast. I wrote that I had found my fortune in gold and had no need for all the newfound wealth. I felt that I would like to share some of it with them. I wrote the address to my old house on the front of the envelope, along with their name. I didn't write a return address, as I didn't have one. I signed the note, "From your old friend."

After placing the note in the envelope, along with the bank draft, I sealed it shut. I returned the clerk's pen and thanked him for the use of it. I then asked him where I could take the letter so that it would be delivered to the East Coast. He told me that if I hurried I could get it on a ship that was heading that way later tonight. He told me of a place that collected all the mail that was to be shipped to other ports.

I wasted no time in locating that collection point, depositing my letter, and paying the fee. They told me that it should arrive at its destination in approximately a month. That didn't surprise me one bit.

I left for my hotel and cleaned up for my trip over to the eatery. When I was done with my meal, I went back to the hotel. It was my plan to get out of this city as fast as I could, as it reminded me too much of what I had left back on the East Coast. I packed all my gear, settled up with the clerk, and then left for the livery. When I arrived, I settled up with the liveryman, loaded all my gear, and then mounted up and headed out with no regrets. I had accomplished all that I had set out to do when I left the pool of gold.

It was dark when I reached my last campsite that I had used on the way there. I ate jerky and pan biscuits, and then washed it down with coffee. When I was finished, I turned in. It was my plan to ride long and hard towards my pool of gold the next morning. For some unknown reason, I had a sense of urgency to get there.

When my alarm went off, I rose without hesitation, took out some jerky and a couple of biscuits, and ate them. I once again washed them down with water. I saddled my mount and placed the packs on the burro. In no time at all, I was on my way towards my pool of gold. It was a long, hot ride, but I had covered a lot of ground. It seemed that everything I was doing now was ritualistic, in that it was the same old thing day in and day out—sleep, breakfast, ride, dinner, and sleep some more.

Time seemed to be flying by. I have no idea just how long I had been on the trail, but it was beginning to feel like forever. I finally reached Lone Pine in the darkness of night. I went to the livery with the intent of trying to make amends with the liveryman. A man came out to me and asked what he could do for me. I asked to see the old liveryman. He told me that he was the new owner. I asked him what had happened to the old one. He said that a man who everyone knew as Long Knife got into a heated argument with him, and when the liveryman went to swing a hammer at Long Knife, he drew his knife and slit the liveryman across the belly. He went on to say that one of the settlement folks walked up, saw it all happening, and thought Long knife was robbing the liveryman, so he shot him. He finished by saying both men later died of their wounds.

I went into shock. I stabled my horse and burro, and then picked up my gear and went to the hotel to take a room for the night. I might just as well have ridden on, as I didn't get a wink of sleep all night.

When I got up and checked out of the hotel, I went over to the livery and loaded up the animals. Once I was ready to ride, I felt a hunger pang, so I decided to ride over to the eatery and put down a meal. Once my belly was full, I mounted up and headed for my camp by the pool of gold. It was a long, hot day in the saddle, but I finally arrived in the late evening. After carefully checking around for intruders, I was satisfied that all was well, so settled in with a grateful appreciation. It hit me that I had failed to supply up while in Lone Pine. That angered me a little. How could I be so forgetful? I decided that I would work the pool of gold until what little supplies I had were depleted and forced me to head over to Beatty to resupply.

I began the next morning working the pool of gold, and did so for the next five days. I wanted to replace all the gold that I had taken on my trip to the West Coast. It was now time for my trip to Beatty. When I rose to my alarm, I wasted no time placing the packs on the burro and saddling my horse. I mounted up and began my trek.

Two days later, I arrived at Beatty. I was going to set camp just outside of the settlement, but instead rode on in and went to the stable. The liveryman met me by the blacksmith shop. I told him to replace the shoes on my burro. He asked me if I wanted my horse's shoes replaced as well. I told him that I was going to sell him, and the next owner could put them on. That perked his ears up. I turned and left for the mercantile.

After purchasing all my supplies and setting them on the boardwalk, I returned to the blacksmith shop to see if the burro was ready to go. He hadn't even started on it yet. He said he wanted to talk about my horse. I told him that we would talk about the horse as soon as he had the shoes on the burro. That visibly aggravated him. I turned and left for the eatery.

When my belly was full, I returned to the blacksmith's shop. He was standing there with a sly grin on his face. I knew he was up to something. He must have felt he had me over a barrel or something, as he told me he would put shoes on my burro as soon as we talked about my horse. I took the lead rope on the burro and mounted my horse. I then told him that he wasn't the only blacksmith around and started to leave. He yelled out to me, asking how much I wanted for my horse.

I yelled back over my shoulder, "Fifty dollars!" He started screaming for me to wait up as he ran after me.

I just rode on over to the mercantile and loaded my supplies. The blacksmith arrived just as I mounted up to leave. He was panting like a dog, out of breath from running. He yelled out that he would buy the horse. I told him that I had sold it to a man in the mercantile, and the man was going to come get the horse over in Lone Pine, where I was going to have shoes put on the burro. He yelled for me to wait a minute as he ran into the mercantile. I turned and was riding off when he came running back out, shaking his fist at me and saying that there wasn't anybody in the mercantile. I just laughed and kept on riding. He was still shaking his fist at me as I rode on out of sight.

I set camp at an old spot up on the trail where I had camped before. It was a well-secluded spot. I could see the trail below. I didn't want to take a chance on that angry liveryman catching up to me, if he indeed did come.

I no more than just settled in for the night when, sure enough, the liveryman came riding up the trail. When he was just about to ride by my camp, I jumped out from behind and yelled out to him. It scared the living hell out of him. He went to draw his firearm, and stopped when he recognized that I had my .44 aimed right at him. He started stuttering and stammering, and finally said that there was no need for violence, as all he wanted was to buy my horse. I told him he was a liar, but we could talk anyway. He asked me how much I wanted for the horse. I told him that the horse wasn't for sale until I sold the saddle. He asked me how much I wanted for the saddle. I told him three hundred dollars. He yelled back that there wasn't any saddle worth that kind of money. I told him that this one was.

He was fuming. He told me that it was highway robbery. I just grinned and told him that it was my price, take it or leave it. He knew I was serious. He shelled out the three hundred, but I could see it was killing him to do so. He wasted no time at all and offered me a hundred dollars for the horse. I walked over, took my saddlebags off the saddle, carried the saddle over to him, and threw it on the ground by him. I told him he could pick his saddle up and leave after that insult. He then offered me two hundred dollars. I reached down and took the safety thong loose from my .44. He threw his arms in the air and yelled that there was no need for violence, as all he wanted to do was buy the horse.

He asked me how much I wanted. He already had three hundred dollars invested, and really needed the horse to get his money back. I told him that if he argued one more time about the price of my horse he could just ride on down the trail without it, no matter how much he offered for it. He knew I was serious. I looked him in the eye with a cold,

Vanishing Anger

hard look, and through gritted teeth told him four hundred dollars or ride on down the trail. He was shaking with rage. I thought I was going to have to kill him.

After a minute of standoff, he reached for his pocket and began shelling out the four hundred dollars. His hands were visibly shaking as he did so. He handed me the money, and I handed the reins to him. I told him not to look back, or his marker would be found along side of the trail. I withdrew my .44 and let it hang down by my side. He dismounted, saddled up the horse, and then remounted and rode off without looking back. All I thought as the liveryman was riding out of sight was, *Now we're even!* I chuckled, and then packed up camp and left.

Chapter Nineteen

I walked all night until I reached where the old prospector was buried. It was daybreak when I arrived. I made breakfast and settled in for a stay that would last another two days. I was physically and mentally exhausted. As I sat there, the thought of Long Knife came to mind. I felt that when my prospecting days came to an end, I just might head up to where the cabin was that he and I built together. It would be a great place to spend my remaining days.

That uneasy feeling suddenly came over me again. This time it was really unsettling me. Something just plain wasn't right. I thought maybe it might have something to do with that blacksmith, but I shook that off, as he would have no idea where to start looking for me.

The next two days went by with that same uneasy feeling coming over me from time to time. When I finally packed up and was ready to return to the pool of gold, the burro had a mind of its own and led me over to where the old prospector was buried. When we arrived by the grave, the burro began braying over and over. That uneasy feeling really returned then. It was so hard that I had to sit down. I started shaking uncontrollably. The burro was still braying away. I couldn't lay my finger on what the hell it was that someone or something was trying to tell me. The air about me became so chilly that I almost had to put my coat on. I thought to myself, *What the hell is it?*

I finally turned to the old prospector's grave and blurted out, "Are you trying to tell me something, old man?"

The burro stopped braying and never did it again while we were there. I sat there intently listening, hoping for an answer. After some time went by and no answer came back from the grave, I got up and led the burro away towards the pool of gold. I arrived as dusk was setting in. I checked around and found everything in order. I offloaded the burro and picketed it in its usual place for the night. I stoked up a fire and placed a pot of coffee on. I then cooked up a venison steak and some potatoes, along with some carrots that I had picked up in Beatty. I ate and just sat by the fire enjoying my coffee. I turned in after several hours had past.

It was a peaceful night of sleep. I built up a fire, and then checked the burro to make sure things were all right with it. After I returned to the fire, I made up the coffee and placed the pot on the fire. I cooked up some pancakes and sausage. It was a great breakfast.

I stayed around camp all day, sorting things out and thinking out my plans for the future. The more I thought about Long Knife's cabin, the more I became convinced that there was where I would spend my remaining days. I decided that I would work the pool of gold two more weeks, and then make my move to that location. I was excited about that.

I had more gold than I would ever need. It was a fortune by anybody's standard. I figured that I had enough that I could have moved back to the East Coast, built a huge mansion on several hundred acres of land, and hired numerous servants to see to all my needs. I thought, *No, that's not for me.* Long Knife's cabin was as luxurious as I would ever desire.

I began working the pool of gold the next morning, and after a week of doing so, I decided to make a trip over to Lone Pine. I packed all the items that I wouldn't be needing anymore at this location and left early the next morning. I arrived at the cabin just as it was turning to dusk on the second day. I was grateful that nobody had discovered the place, as it was just as Long Knife had left it. I went in and lit up the lanterns. I offloaded the burro and turned it loose in the corral. The burro really liked that freedom. I placed everything in its proper place. The cabin was much more magnificent than I had remembered.

I would return to Lone Pine in the morning to stock up on everything that I would need to get started out in my retirement home after another week at the pool of gold. I had brought a large amount of gold with me, but I wouldn't be needing it for quite some time, as I still had a great deal of money left from all my horse trading. I sought out and found a place to hide the gold. It was so well hidden that nobody would ever be able to find it. I was proud of myself.

The next morning, I made breakfast, cooking it on the hearth. That sure beat holding a skillet over an open fire. The steak and eggs were good. I then placed the packboards on the burro and went down to Lone Pine and stocked up so I could begin my life of retirement in my new home. I would pick up the supplies that I needed for my stay at the pool of gold on my way back down the next time.

I went to the livery and had the new blacksmith put new shoes on my burro. We became better acquainted, and that was good, as we would be seeing much more of each other in the near future. While he worked on the shoes, I walked over to the eatery and had some coffee, along with a large piece of apple pie, while waiting. I thought to myself, *I'll be doing this much more often in the future.* Damn that pie was good! My mouth watered for more, but I had to use common sense and get out of there.

When I arrived at the livery, the blacksmith was finished, so I paid up and left for home. I really liked the sound of that—home! It had a nice ring to it. When I arrived, I offloaded all the supplies and placed them all in their proper places.

I spent the next two weeks at the cabin, enjoying all that it had to offer. The scenery was magnificent. I killed an elk and prepared all the meat for future use. I stretched the hide on a drying rack that Long Knife had built. He sure had things there in order for comfortable living. I would be forever grateful for the opportunity to have met Long Knife and truly find a friend in him. Friends in this country were hard to come by.

I spent the next week bringing in enough wood to last for a long time. Hay for the burro was the next task that I tackled. I completed that job over the course of the next couple of days. I was now ready to spend my last week at the pool of gold before returning to the cabin to retire.

I rose early the next morning to make the trek over to my pool. I ate pan biscuits and jerky, as I didn't want to waste any time getting back to my campsite. I packed everything I would need to sustain myself while I was there. It consisted of, what else, biscuits and jerky, along with coffee to wash it all down. I knew I would get tired of it, but also knew that there would be better waiting for me on my return to my piece of paradise. I closed everything up and left for the pool.

It was late on the second day when I arrived. I removed the packs from the burro, and then picketed it for the night. I built a fire and made coffee. I then cooked an elk steak that I had stuck in my pack at the last minute. It was good. I turned in early, as I wanted to get started as soon as I was up and ready in the morning.

Each day became ritualistic as the week wore on. Jerky, biscuits, coffee, and I became good friends. Each morning I placed the packboards on the burro's back, loaded with a pack on one side with my food and coffee, along with a canteen of water hanging on one of the cross members of the pack frame. My shovel, pick, bucket, and lantern were hanging on the other side of the pack frame. I would gather as many nuggets as I could readily see with the naked eye, and then shovel some of the gravel into my bucket for panning out over the campfire in the evening. I would always get another ounce to ounce and a half of gold out of each bucket.

On the fourth day, I had a visitor that shook things up around there for a couple of hours. I heard the burro braying in a strange manner, so I walked outside of the campsite and was startled to see another cougar standing just outside the opening. I withdrew my .44 and emptied it into the cat. I'm sure its sights were set on my burro. After examining the animal, I decided that the hide was too riddled to keep, after six bullets had passed through it. I dragged it away from camp a distance, and left it for the vultures that would in all certainty show up to devour its carcass.

I went back into the campsite and settled down the burro with a handful of grain. I felt an urge to pack up and leave, but I decided to stay the course and spend one more day gathering gold. I had already buried everything that I had gathered during the first four days, deep under the sand on the far side of the spring. After sprinkling dry sand over the top of the place the gold was buried, you would be hard challenged to ever find it. It was tucked just back under some of the low pine boughs. It was a goodly sum of gold. I would take all the gold with me that I gathered the next day. All the buried gold would make a nice bank for when I ever felt I needed some.

The next morning rolled around and I headed for the pool of gold. When I entered the canyon, the burro acted strange and tried to pull back from continuing. I thought there might be another cougar in there, so I encouraged the burro to come along. When I was about halfway in towards the pool, the ground shook hard. A large boulder about three feet across struck me from the back, knocking me forward and settling on my waist and legs. I was pinned, and there was no way I could budge that boulder. When I fell, the burro ran off a ways and wouldn't come near me. It just stood there braying away like nothing I ever heard before.

After several hours had past, I felt the life draining out of me. The burro finally came over and nuzzled my face. It stood there until my eyes slowly closed and darkness overcame my awareness.

The pool of gold is still there for someone to find. It's been a good ride.

Review Requested:
If you loved this book, would you please provide
a review at Amazon.com?
Thank You

CPSIA information can be obtained
at www.ICGtesting.com
Printed in the USA
FSHW02n0454140718
50288FS